Mandelb

A FRACTAL STORY

NOAH A CLAWSON

Copyright © 2022 by Noah A. Clawson All Rights Reserved.

ISBN: 979-8-4132-5391-5

No part of this publication may be reproduced, distributed, or transmitted in any form or by any means, including photocopying, recording, or other electronic or mechanical methods, or by any information storage and retrieval system without the prior written permission of the publisher, except in the case of very brief quotations embodied in critical reviews and certain other noncommercial uses permitted by copyright law

This book was published thanks to free support and training from:

TCKPublishing.com

DEDICATION

This book is dedicated to Felix whose magical spirit left this earth way too soon. In his short life, he lived the chaos of creativity, understood the interconnectedness of life, and appreciated the beauty of the avant-garde.

Contents

OFFSHOOT ONE: GREGOR   1

Root 1.1- Gregor's Dream of Smoke   pg 3

Root 1.2- The Purple Goat   pg 11

Root 1.3- The Pipe That Gregor Smokes   pg 15

Root 1.4- Gregor's Last Day at Black Gold   pg 17

Root 1.5- Before Black Gold   pg 29

    rootlet 1.51- what happened in Rockafella   pg 36

    rootlet 1.52- the effects of the lotus cigar   pg 44

    rootlet 1.53- Gregor follows his instincts   pg 47

    rootlet 1.54- Gregor meets Bacchus   pg 50

    rootlet 1.55- Gregor remembers bits and pieces   pg 54

OFFSHOOT TWO: ENTROPIS   59

Root 2.1- Gregor Meets Entropis   pg 61

Root 2.2- The Cane of Chaos   pg 67

Root 2.3- The End of Gregor   pg 75

OFFSHOOT THREE: MANDELBROT   78

Root 3.1- Hectic Norder Meets Mandelbrot   pg 81

Root 3.2- Mandelbrot Reveals His Past   pg 85

Root 3.3- Mandelbrot's Struggle to Master Nature   pg 101

Root 3.4- How Mandelbrot Became Sick   pg 107

OFFSHOOT FOUR: THE BOWELS   113

Root 4.1-Belt 87, RP Cards, K12 Numbers, & the H5f   pg 115

Root 4.2- Hectic Gets the Runaround   pg 125

    rootlet 4.21- the registration office   pg 133

    rootlet 4.22- Mr. Tantalus   pg 141

    rootlet 4.23- Hectic receives a K12 card   pg 148

    rootlet 4.24- Sector 92, Quadrant 71, Section g187   pg 155

Root 4.3 - The Chamber of Belts   pg 163

    rootlet 4.31- the badger   pg 170

    rootlet 4.32- trouble in the CB   pg 172

    rootlet 4.33- the trouble worsens   pg 178

Root 4.4 - Dr Sisyphus   pg 183

    rootlet 4.41- The Bowels   pg 190

    rootlet 4.42- the chamber of directions   pg 195

    rootlet 4.43- the end of Sisyphus   pg 205

Root 4.5- Red Rage   pg 213

Root 4.6- The Hydra   pg 217

Root 4.7- The Light to the Top   pg 223

OFFSHOOT FIVE: HECTIC MEETS INCHOATE   225

Root 5.1- The Swim   pg 227

Root 5.2- Inchoate Regurgitates Hectic   pg 229

Root 5.3- Inchoate's Last Rebirth   pg 231

Root 5.4- Inchoate's Process   pg 235

Root 5.5- Hints of Mandelbrot   pg 239

Root 5.6- Hectic Remembers Mandelbrot   pg 245

Root 5.7- Inchoate Spins a Yarn   pg 251

    rootlet 5.71- Yellow   pg 251

    rootlet 5.72- the valley animals   pg 259

    rootlet 5.73- the learning place   pg 268

Root 5.8- Inchoate Performs Brain Surgery on Hectic   pg 283

OFFSHOOT SIX: THE WAY BACK TO GREGOR   289

    Root 6.1- Frustration, Energy, and Gregor   pg 291

        rootlet 6.11- the genealogy of frustration   pg 291

        rootlet 6.12- creative energy   pg 292

        rootlet 6.13- economic energy   pg 295

        rootlet 6.14- political energy   pg 302

        rootlet 6.15- Inchoate's alternative energy idea   pg 309

OFFSHOOT SEVEN: THE MANDELBROT SET   317

ACKNOWLEDGMENTS

I want to thank my girlfriend, Libby Brow, for convincing me that this book had value and that I should publish it. Despite having many personal challenges, she spent countless hours preparing this book for publication. Without her selfless dedication, this book would have never made it off my computer. I would also like to thank her sister, Sarah Brow-Hill, for the many hours she spent creating the artwork for the front cover of this novel, her dad, David Brow for my author photos, and her mom, Jill Brow, for her enthusiastic support. I would like to thank Stona Fitch of the Concord Free Press for his advice and encouraging me to self-publish. Additionally, I would like to thank my friend, Phil Maret, for listening to my off-the-wall ideas for so many years. Without his support, I may have lost my mind. Finally, I'd like to thank my brother, Larry, for late night help with formatting, and my mother for coming up with the name Hectic Norder as one of the names for my main character.

OFFSHOOT ONE

GREGOR

Root 1.1 – Gregor's Dream of Smoke, Sisyphus, and the Bug

At first, Gregor saw only gray. Then tiny black specks emerged. The specks began to expand as if they were marks on a rubber sheet stretching outward in all directions. The gray suddenly diffused into smoke that unfurled into the blackness. Some of the smoke wisps danced slowly around each other like ballroom dancers. These wisps drew ever closer until they formed pewter-like droplets that immediately fell from Gregor's view. The wisps that remained in the ballroom of blackness used the extra space to dance faster. They twirled in ever-widening circles until they spun out of Gregor's sight. Only two long sinuous wisps remained. The wisps intertwined around Gregor and formed a double helix.

The helix began to contract around Gregor in a pulsating rhythm. In the darkness, a yellow pinprick appeared. With each contraction, the yellow light grew bigger. An intense flurry of contractions expelled Gregor out of the darkness and into the light.

He felt a hard surface against his knees and heard the sound of waves breaking upon a shore. Gregor was in a fetal position with his eyes closed. He opened his eyes and unfurled like a sprout reaching for the sun. Fully upright, he stood on a massive boulder that overlooked the entrance of a gulf. In the gulf's leaden water floated charcoal-colored debris that resembled either flagella or sheets of membrane. On the land surrounding the gulf, massive billows of thick smoke slowly churned. Gregor witnessed the billows gradually solidify into great slate-colored mountains that remained fixed in form.

An itch flared up in Gregor's belly button. He went to scratch, but a gray cord that extended from his belly to the black sky above blocked his fingers. Gregor worked his pinky into the tight space between the cord and his stomach. Out jumped a black bug. The bug began secreting an iridescent substance and scuttled up the cord. Vibrant colors infused up the cord after the bug in interweaving strands. As the psychedelic threads reached the sky, the long cord connected to Gregor's belly evaporated. The colors branched into the blackness and blanketed the sky in an arabesque pattern. Within the chromatic whorls, the black bug grew until he occupied the middle third of the sky

The giant bug rumbled and spat a series of blue lightning bolts at the gulf. Each strike infused a blue tinge that slowly turned the gray gulf steely. After a bit, the bug stopped and shrank away. The color swirls pushed into the empty space he had left behind and began to coalesce. The yellows merged into a saffron sun, and the blues merged into the sky. The steely sea absorbed the sky's light and turned Prussian blue.

The debris floating in the water melded together into amorphous blobs, and the blobs undulated through the gulf like umbrellas opening and closing. Then the sun began to shine with searing intensity and the ocean receded. The blue water evaporated into gray smoke and expanded into nothingness. Soon the gulf was completely dry.

The receding water left behind the amorphous blobs. Gregor noticed that the blobs were actually jellyfish-like creatures with the eyes of children. They fixed their gazes on Gregor as if they were pleading with him to save their lives. Most of the jellies died and dissipated into smoke that dissolved into the gray landscape. The surviving fish flopped off the rocks and away from where the ocean had deserted them. Gregor followed the flopping fish. He noticed that some of the fish had evolved stubby little legs that they used to negotiate the terrain. The stubby-legged fish that continued to press forward evolved into frogs. Gregor followed the frogs. The frogs eventually evolved into lizards, and the lizards eventually evolved into mammals. Gregor was soon walking amid a great caravan of mammals. Directly around him, were mostly Gorillas, orangutans, chimpanzees, and bonobos. Amongst them, he was the only one who walked fully upright. Out of the great blur of bodies, Gregor could see the elephants and giraffes towering above the others. Towards the front, Gregor thought he could make out woolly mammoths and saber-tooth tigers.

Suddenly he smelled coffee. He looked around and noticed that the evolving animals he had been following were gone. Ahead of him, he saw a shiny mountain. As he continued forward, he saw that the mountain was actually a vast metallic structure. The structure consisted of several steely cylinders together in a cluster. A jumble of pipes wrapped around the cylinders in an intricate network. Interspersed among the pipes were numerous gears that interacted with each other at varied angles. The gears appeared to power several clocks with hands that moved at different speeds. Some of the clocks had hands that appeared not to move at all, while others spun in a dizzying blur. On a few of the clocks, the hour hand rotated quickly, while the minute hand stayed still. In the center of the structure was the oddest clock of all. The clock had four hands. Two of the hands rotated clockwise, while the other two rotated counter-clockwise. The four hands switched direction and speed as Gregor watched.

A moat of percolating coffee surrounded the structure, and in front of the moat was a large shiny desk covered with stacks of paper. Also on the desk was a percolator with a bell-shaped glass knob for the coffee to percolate through. On top of the knob was a tiny little handle. Gregor pulled gently on the handle, which caused the knob to detach from the percolator and make a surprisingly loud ringing sound.

Immediately, the odd clock increased in speed. The four hands moved in violent jerking motions as if disharmonious forces were directing their movement. Suddenly, they exploded off the clock and spun away like a propeller that had snapped off a flying helicopter. A column of smoke effused from a hole in the clock's center and arched to the desk like a rainbow. When the smoke hit the desk, the papers flew into the air. The smoke and papers churned rapidly together like the water at the base of a gigantic waterfall.

The churning mass exploded, and in the air where the smoke and papers had churned was a man comprised entirely of paper. The paper man floated gently down into a swivel chair that was behind the desk. His face looked wrinkled and marred like paper that had been crumpled and flattened out again. What little hair he had on his balding head was frizzy, like the ragged ends of pages torn from notebooks. Two horizontal commas joined at their heads under his nose and formed a mustache. On his chin was a beard of exclamation points and question marks. Large sheets of paper extended from his torso and folded into a suit embedded with numerous envelopes that formed various sized pockets. The paper man's core body was white and contrasted with his suit-like extension, which was dark with densely typed letters. Gregor could hear the delicate sound of paper crumpling as the paper man shifted slightly in his seat.

"Hello, I am Dr. Sisyphus, professor of economics. Did you ring the bell?" the man of paper asked.

"Yes, I rang the bell," said Gregor.

"Well, what can I do for you sir?"

"I feel very tired," said Gregor. "I would like—"

"Oh hold on for a second," interrupted Sisyphus as he shot up to his feet. He patted his suit like someone searching for their keys. Eventually, he pulled a smoking pipe and a small glass vial from one of his pockets. The vial contained black ink, which he carefully poured into the bowl of his pipe. He put the pipe's mouthpiece to his papery lips and inhaled the ink with a loud slurp. He then sat back down in his chair, put his hands behind his head, and began blowing ink bubbles out of his mouth. As hundreds of bubbles drifted through the air, he pointed his pipe at Gregor and asked, "What can I do for you?"

"I need a cup of coffee to help me wake up," Gregor said.

"Naturally," replied Sisyphus. "Just give me your coffee drinking papers."

Gregor peered at Sisyphus. "I do not have any coffee drinking papers," Gregor said. "I just—"

Bang! The ink bubbles exploded. At 4:15 AM, Gregor woke from his dream and began rubbing his bald head. He had been dreaming of Sisyphus every night for the past few weeks.

Prior to that, he had dreamt of Sisyphus only once, but that was many years ago.

ROOT 1.2 – THE PURPLE GOAT

Bang! The ink bubbles exploded. At 4:15 AM, Gregor woke from his dream and ran his hand through his thick unkempt hair. He had forty five minutes to get to the Purple Goat Café. He arrived for his opening shift ten minutes early and saw that his manager was already in the store. Gregor was surprised; Bacchus was a laid-back guy who often came to work late and hung-over. Bacchus saw Gregor arrive and went outside to greet him.

"Hey boss man," said Gregor. "What are you doing here so early?"

"Got a call from corporate last night," he said. "They're tripling all the prices of our beverages."

"Tripling! Are they nuts?!"

"Dude, no yelling in the morning. Chill," said Bacchus as he lit a cigarette. "Would you like a ciggy?"

"I don't smoke."

"Well you should. Smoke might bring you balance. Just look at your shirt."

Gregor was wearing a long black shirt. Half of the shirt was tattered and covered in dirt, while the other half seemed to be in perfect condition.

"Forget about balance and think about our customers!" snapped Gregor

"There's no need to freak out," Bacchus assured him. "Apparently, there have been a few minor glitches in our coffee delivery network; however, corporate has arranged for us to receive an emergency shipment at two o'clock this afternoon."

"That's absurd! We serve most of our customers before two!"

"You've got to chill," said Bacchus through a smoky exhalation. "We're only talking about coffee here. As soon as the shipment comes, we will un-triple our prices back to what they were before. Anyone who cannot afford this temporary price spike can return this afternoon. In the meantime, please allow me to dissipate your troubles with my fail-safe therapy for uptightness." Bacchus took a deep drag on his cigarette, and began to move his eyes in the most mysterious manner. His right eye rolled rightward at a rather rapid rate, while his left eye looped leftward at a somewhat slower pace. The middle of his mouth crimped; yet, the corners were open wide. His mouth looked like an hourglass tipped over to the side. From his mouth's corners came smoke in snuffs and puffs that unfurled into the air like wispy mustache tufts. The tension on Gregor's face broke and he began to smile.

Bacchus suddenly adopted a somber demeanor. "Uh-oh," he said. "Some uptightness has formed within me that I must immediately dissipate." Bacchus stuck out his rear and emitted a deep resonating fart. "Dissipate away," he bellowed. Gregor burst into laughter. Bacchus' therapy had worked.

After Bacchus finished another cigarette, he and Gregor entered The Purple Goat to prepare for the 6:00 AM opening. At 5:53 AM, they donned their purple aprons and decided to open a few minutes early. Bacchus went to fire up the store's espresso machine—the Byzantina, while Gregor opened the front doors. The Byzantina was a vast metallic structure consisting of several steely cylinders adjoined together in a cluster. A jumble of pipes wrapped around the cylinders in an intricate network. Interspersed among the pipes were numerous gears that interacted with each other at varied angles. Bacchus pulled down on a power lever; the

Byzantina hissed and belched to life. Thick black smoke effused from the machine's venting shafts, filled the café, and blinded Gregor.

"Bacchus, what the hell are you doing?" asked Gregor. Bacchus did not reply. From somewhere outside the store, a familiar rumbling began to intensify. A trucker, and one of Gregor's regulars, pulled his eighteen-wheeler into the parking lot. The trucker had been working very long hours and was in desperate need of some coffee.

ROOT 1.3 — THE PIPE THAT GREGOR SMOKES

Gregor stopped rubbing his bald head, rose from bed, and exited the cave into the valley. He lit his pipe and began smoking under the massive tree in the courtyard center. The pipe was a gift from Bacchus when Gregor first came to the valley about fifteen years prior. Bacchus had led Gregor from the valley into the cave, which Gregor then made his home.

In the dim light from Bacchus' torch, Gregor had seen a root protruding from the stone ceiling. Bacchus had looked at Gregor and said, "That root is from the tree in the valley. Only a tree looking for the truth would send a root this deep. Gregor, I think this root would make an excellent pipe for you." Bacchus cut a piece of the root from the ceiling, and several days later presented Gregor with the pipe.

The pipe had two stems and a bowl with two cavities that were connected in the middle with a narrow slit. Bacchus had carved the stems into two snakes, and the bowl into a grimacing goat's head. The snakes' intertwining bodies fused at their ends into one tail and one head. The goat's grimacing mouth crimped in the middle and formed the unique double-bowled pipe. When Gregor inhaled on the snakes' tails, the goat's mouth glowed like a fiery hourglass. After each inhalation, one thread of smoke would snake upward from each cavity. The two threads of smoke converged over the double bowl and intertwined upward into the darkness.

Gregor had lived in the cave and worked at the Black Gold coffee station for a long time. Unfortunately, Gregor lost his job a few weeks ago when Black Gold ran out of coffee. After Gregor lost his job, he began to have the dream of smoke every time he went to bed. The dream seemed to jolt Gregor out of the insect-like state he had been in for many years. When he awoke in the morning, his mind would spin with questions. Lately, he had been wondering why there had never been any indication that coffee supplies were low.

ROOT 1.4--GREGOR'S LAST DAY AT BLACK GOLD

On the very day the coffee ran out, Gregor woke up and smelled smoke. When he arrived at work later that morning, he found thick black smoke enveloping the station. Gregor's manager, Ludwig Boltzmann, was over by the coffee pumps talking to a man in a shiny suit. Initially, all Gregor could see was the distinct silhouette of his manager, Ludwig, leaning on his walking cane, which he always had with him.

Only when Gregor came closer did he see that Ludwig was talking to the man wearing the shiny suit and smoking a cigar. When the shiny suit man saw Gregor approaching, he wheeled around and vigorously shook Gregor's hand.

"Howdy," he said. "I'm your regional manager Kappy Lism." Kappy had a gigantic smile, which seemed like a permanent feature of his well-tanned face. His cigar was as big as a submarine sandwich and effused smoke like a coal-burning power plant. "You don't mind if I smoke?" he asked Gregor.

"Not at all," said Gregor.

"Super!" said Kappy, as he reached into his vest and pulled out a second cigar. Kappy lit the second cigar with the first and began smoking both at the same time. He somehow managed to speak with the cigars sticking from the corners of his mouth like walrus tusks.

"Hell of a job you guys are doing," he said. "I just wanted to personally congratulate the both of you." Kappy inhaled on both cigars and blew some smoke billows into the air. "With you two here, I won't have to worry about the slight complications that may arise this morning."

"What kind of complications?" asked Ludwig.

"You might be a little bit short on coffee today," replied Kappy.

"How can that be?" asked Gregor. "We were never short on coffee before."

"How?" said Kappy. "I'll tell you how. An ongoing civil war in Africa has damaged many of our coffee plantations. In Indonesia, radical extremists have destroyed twenty of our refineries. Two days ago, one of our tankers struck a reef and spilled fifteen million barrels of coffee into the ocean. My friend, we are weathering the perfect storm of unfortunate instances."

"Do you think we will run out of coffee?" asked Ludwig. Kappy inhaled deeply and blew another huge billow into the air.

"Don't worry Ludwig," said Kappy confidently. "I have tripled the prices of all our coffee beverages." Ludwig and Gregor looked at the prices displayed on the coffee pumps. The various coffees, which had always cost around a dollar fifty a gallon, were now around four-fifty a gallon.

"Kappy you can't raise prices that high," said Ludwig emphatically. "Our customers depend on us for cheap energy to get them through the day. I doubt most of them can even afford three dollars a gallon. The sudden price increase will cause chaos."

"I assure you that there is nothing to worry about," said Kappy. "I have arranged for more coffee to arrive at this station this afternoon. Anyone who can't afford coffee this morning can return later when the prices go back down. I think once the customers see the situation they will understand."

A rumbling noise emanated from off in the distance. "I think I hear your first customers coming," said Kappy. "I'm going to go back to corporate headquarters now and let you boys get to work. I will check back in with you this afternoon." As an eighteen-wheeler pulled into the station, Kappy slipped away into the smoke and vanished.

A trucker, who ordered sixty gallons of coffee a day, pulled into the station. He always pumped the coffee into a barrel-sized thermos, which he kept hitched to the underside of his truck. A straw-like pipe delivered the coffee from the thermos into the truck's cab. A pacifier capped the end of the pipe, which the man had been sucking on when he pulled into the station. The man let the truck idle in the lot for a bit, while he continued to suckle on the coffee nipple. He eventually finished nursing and got out of the truck. When he went to pump himself some coffee, he noticed the increased prices. He turned to Gregor and said, "Hey buddy, your coffee prices are set wrong."

"Actually," said Gregor, "those prices are correct. We had to raise prices because we had a problem with our coffee delivery system."

"Raise prices!" the man hollered. "You didn't just raise prices, you tripled them."

"Don't worry," said Gregor. "The prices are going to drop back down to a dollar fifty this afternoon when we receive our coffee shipment. Why don't you just return then?"

The man pointed at the truck and said, "I need to deliver this shipment to the warehouse by One o'clock today. If I don't, my boss won't pay me."

"Okay, if you explain the situation to your boss, I am sure he will understand," replied Gregor.

The man shook his head and said, "My employer depends on me to meet specific deadlines. If I don't, he will go out of business and I will have no job. Moreover, my contract states that I will not receive pay for late deliveries. The past week has been especially difficult for me. I only made my deadlines by continually drinking diesel blend to keep me awake. I have not slept for six days. If I do not get a refill this morning, I will fall asleep and miss my afternoon deadline."

"I'm really sorry sir," said Gregor. "I don't have the authority to change prices."

The man took a deep breath and said, "Look, I am a regular customer. Just for this morning, can you make an exception and charge me the old price of a dollar fifty a gallon?"

"Let me ask my manager," said Gregor. Gregor looked over at Ludwig, who was busy talking to an incensed woman in a station wagon. "Hey Ludwig!" he yelled. "Can we charge our regular customers the old price just for today?"

"Yea," yipped the woman in the station wagon. "You should charge your regular customers the old price."

"All our customers are regular customers," said Ludwig. "If I charge all the regular customers a dollar fifty, we will be out of coffee in an hour." The woman's eyes widened with shock. She took a cell phone from her purse and dialed a number.

"Black Gold will be out of coffee in an hour!" she shrieked into the phone.

"That is not what I said," said Ludwig. "I said if we didn't raise prices we would run out in an hour."

"Did I hear that you are going to be out of coffee in an hour?" interjected a man in a convertible.

"No!" said Ludwig. "Only if—"

"Never mind only if," said the man. "Just fill my thermos to the brim." As Ludwig filled the man's thermos, the man made a call on his cell phone. "Black Gold will be out of coffee in an hour," he said into the receiver.

In fifteen minutes, a line of customers formed that stretched from the station to the horizon. Meanwhile, the smoke that was hovering above the station had slowly begun to sink. The sinking smoke branched towards the ground like the roots from a huge tree. Within an hour, the smoke was turning in slow vortices along the ground like the waters of a great gray ocean. Although Gregor could not see in the gray smoke, he worked very efficiently. He had worked in the station long enough that he did not need to see. All the behaviors of being a coffee station attendant had become instinct for him. He moved unconsciously through the smoke like a jellyfish drifting through an ocean.

After an hour of work, the sound of Ludwig's voice blaring from the intercom jarred Gregor back into consciousness.

"Attention valued customers," said Ludwig. "We are temporarily out of coffee. More coffee will arrive this afternoon.

Please come back then." Thousands of angry voices rumbled from the smoke like resonating thunder.

Gregor felt something poke his back. He turned around and could just make out Ludwig, who was standing only inches from him.

"Come on," said Ludwig. "Let's get out of here."

"Why are we leaving?" said Gregor.

"Our customers are about to be very dissatisfied."

"You mean we are leaving to avoid complaints?" Gregor asked incredulously.

"No," said Ludwig. "We are leaving to avoid being killed."

Ludwig hooked Gregor around the neck with his cane's handle and pulled him to the coffee storage unit behind the station. The unit was a massive steel cylinder, which stood about fifteen stories high. A short ladder on rollers started about ten feet off the ground and extended straight up the cylinder's side to a spiral staircase. Ludwig reached up with his cane and hooked the bottom rung. He rolled the ladder down to the ground like a garage door. "After you," Ludwig said to Gregor. When they reached the stairs, Ludwig rolled the ladder back up behind them.

The stairs wound around the cylinder like a vine growing up a post. Ludwig and Gregor climbed far above the smoke. When they reached the top, the smoke below looked like a great gray ocean. Above them, the sun sent streaks of yellow across a clear blue sky. In the radiant light, Gregor could see clearer than he had in many years. For the first time, he realized how ugly Ludwig really was. He was very tall, sported a goatee, had horrible acne, and was drastically cross-eyed. Yet, Ludwig had a look of wild wisdom to him that was strangely appealing to Gregor.

Ludwig and Gregor remained on the cylinder for many hours. Late that afternoon, the smoke began to dissipate. Down below, Gregor could see hundreds of customers scattered across the ground like beached fish.

"Oh my God!" said Gregor. "Are they dead?"

"No," said Ludwig. "They are suffering from caffeine withdrawal. They lack the energy to get up and leave."

"Are they too weak to get up?"

"Not exactly," said Ludwig. "They are unwilling. Their spirits have crashed and now they are in a great depression."

"What will happen to them?" Gregor asked.

Ludwig looked at Gregor with his wise cross-eyes and said, "Those with the will to survive will adapt to the new environment. The rest will lie there until they die."

"Geez, I hope we receive that coffee delivery soon," said Gregor.

The mobile phone in Ludwig's coat started to make a ringing sound. "Hello," he said as he put the phone to his ear. "Hi Kappy, how are you…? What's the problem…? Oh, I see… Oh, that's very bad… No, I understand… No… No… No… No need for you to feel bad Kappy, sometimes even perfect systems collapse into chaos… I know the decision was hard for you Kappy, and I really appreciate your pity… Good-bye."

Ludwig took the phone from his ear and looked off into space.

"What did Kappy say?" asked Gregor.

"He is laying us off," Ludwig replied.

"Laying us off! How can that be? Does he think we were the ones who messed up the order?"

"Don't worry," said Ludwig. "You are not responsible for messed up order. Messed up order is responsible for you. You need either some coffee or a cigar. Coffee cannot exist without a cigar, and a cigar cannot exist without coffee. Therefore, I am compelled to offer both of them to you."

Ludwig produced a bag of coffee briquettes and a cigar from inside his coat and handed them to Gregor. Gregor was not familiar with the symbols on the cigar band, which read: $\underline{S=K \log W}$. However, he instantly recognized the insignia on the briquette bag as the logo of one of Black Gold's special reserve coffees. The design depicted a man in a business suit running with a spear. He was chasing a green buck with golden antlers that was running towards a murky forest. The words "Green Buck Blend" curved over the top of the insignia in elegant cursive. An inscription under the insignia read: <u>This rich blend is too good to share. Go ahead and pour yourself another cup.</u>

Since the decaffeinated customers didn't look very dangerous, Gregor decided to go home. He thanked Ludwig for the gifts and said goodbye. As Gregor started down the winding stairs, Ludwig was leaning on his cane looking at him with those wise cross-eyes. "Au Revoir Gregor," said Ludwig. "Au Revoir."

ROOT 1.5 — BEFORE BLACK GOLD

Gregor blew more smoke out of his mouth. The smoke formed several wisps, which looked vaguely like squirrel tails. All the leaves on the tree were gone, and the branches were white like the hand of a skeleton sticking from the ground. Recently, Gregor had begun to wonder why he did not notice the construction of a dome over the rift. The only memories he had were meeting Bacchus and his last day at the coffee station. He had begun to wonder if perhaps he was only a wisp of smoke that had swirled only by chance into existence. He wondered if he really had a past at all, or if his impressions of the past were only impressions.

Perhaps two decades ago, Gregor was attending the same college as his girlfriend, Pollyanna. Between semesters, Pollyanna flew to Rockafella, Washington, to visit her Uncle Sam. The last time she saw her uncle, he kept raving about a new coffee shop in town. Since Pollyanna loved coffee, she decided to visit the shop the following morning. The next morning when she entered the shop, she was the only customer in the store. The sole employee was an obese man wearing a black apron over black clothes. He stood next to the register and rested his enormous gut across the counter.

When Pollyanna approached he said, "Good morning—and welcome to Black Gold. I'm Phil Moore. What can I do for you?"

"I'll have your coffee of the day please," Pollyanna said.

On the wall behind Phil were various buttons and a metal handle. Phil switched the handle from the horizontal position to the vertical and pushed one of the buttons. From beneath the counter, he pulled out a hose with a metal nozzle. Phil pulled the trigger on the dispenser with his pudgy pink finger and dispensed coffee into a cup.

"That will be twenty cents," he said as he handed the cup to Pollyanna.

"Only twenty cents," said Pollyanna. "The price on the board says a dollar eighty."

"A dollar eighty is the price of our coffee per gallon," said Phil.

"By the gallon? Who drinks coffee by the gallon?" asked Pollyanna.

"I do. I drink myself one cup and then I fill myself some more."

"Why do you drink that much coffee?"

"Nothing in this world gives me energy like Black Gold coffee. I used to be careful with my caloric intake because I got tired when I gained weight. Ever since I started drinking Black Gold, I have been able to steadily gain weight and still have plenty of energy. I figure the bigger I get the more coffee I can drink." Pollyanna seemed skeptical of Mr. Moore's claims. However, when she drank her coffee she experienced a massive energy burst and sprinted home.

Uncle Sam was waiting for her in the driveway. He asked her if she could help him with a few chores. Pollyanna actually welcomed the suggestion. That day she cleaned Sam's entire house, and chopped enough firewood to last all winter. By the time the coffee wore off, the sun was setting.

Pollyanna was stunned at the amount of work she had completed. "Sam, do you know how productive I would be if I drank that coffee all the time?" Sam looked deep into Pollyanna's eyes.

"Actually," he said, "I have thought about that a great deal. Pollyanna, I want you to listen very carefully to me. Black Gold is going to radically change the world. I know that sounds crazy, which is why I did not tell you about Black Gold before you drank some. I knew that you would believe me only if you had personally experienced Black Gold's energy. Other people will try Black Gold. They will conclude, as you did, that they can exploit Black Gold to exponentially increase their productivity. Businesses will want to utilize Black Gold to secure an insurmountable competitive advantage. They will move their factories to Rockafella, where their employees can drink Black Gold coffee. Rockafella will experience an explosion of economic growth, the shockwaves of which will spread across the world. The day Black Gold opened their door for business, a door in time opened to prosperity. The first to reach prosperity will shut the door behind them. The prosperous will want to protect the tremendous advantage that Black Gold bestows upon them. They will use Black Gold's energy to obtain more advantages. Soon, only two groups of people will exist in the world. There will be one group with all the advantages, and one group with none. Pollyanna, I love you. I pray you become a member of the group with all the advantages."

Pollyanna certainly did not want to live the rest of her life disadvantaged. That night, she called Gregor and told him of what her Uncle had said. She wanted him to come to Rockafella and share with her the opportunity that Black Gold offered. Gregor, however, was very skeptical of her story.

"You know how fanatical Sam gets," he said. "The last time you were in Rockafella he forced you to stay in his house the entire time."

"He didn't force me. At the time, Red Tide virus was gripping Rockafella. Sam told me that contact with an infected person could kill me. I was too afraid to leave the house."

"He made you adhere to a strict diet of hotdogs and apple pie."

"He didn't make me do anything," said Pollyanna. "He simply informed me that the only inoculation for Red Tide was hot dogs and apple pie. I was too afraid to eat any other food."

"Oh please! Hot dogs and apple pie aren't going to prevent any virus."

"Hey, don't knock Uncle Sam's tried and true inoculation. Remember I never got Red Tide."

"That is because Red Tide only exists in your uncle's mind.

"Untrue! Most of the town was infected."

"How do you know? Did you see most of the town?"

"Don't be ridiculous Gregor! You know I was in the house during the outbreak."

"Well then how do you know anybody was sick?"

"The quarantine squad came to my street. They quarantined those two Chinese guys who lived in the pink house with all the flowers. I think they died. I never saw them again."

Pollyanna desperately wanted to share with Gregor the prosperity that Black Gold was offering but could not overcome his skepticism. She decided that she would have to get him to drink Black Gold coffee. The next morning she stopped at a gift shop and bought a one-gallon thermos. The thermos came with an apple-shaped top that unscrewed and doubled as a cup. After stopping at Black Gold to fill the thermos, she caught the first flight back home.

When her plane landed, Gregor was waiting for her in his car. Pollyanna put all her belongings in the back seat except for her thermos. The thermos she kept with her in the passenger seat. As they pulled out of the airport, she unscrewed the apple top. Pollyanna slowly poured the coffee into the apple cup. Tendrils of steam rose from the coffee, intertwined, and entered Gregor's nose.

"That smells heavenly," said Gregor.

Pollyanna raised the cup to his lips. "Drink," she said. Gregor put his pursed lips on the rim of the apple cup, and took a long slurp as fingers of steam caressed his face. Pollyanna put the apple to her own lips and took a sip. Soon Black Gold's energy had possessed them both. "History has opened a window in time for us," Pollyanna said. "Gregor, drive to Rockafella right now."

Normally Gregor would have cringed at the idea of driving five days to Rockafella. Yet, the Black Gold coursing through his veins made a five-day car drive seem desirable. Gregor and Pollyanna took the westward exit and headed cross-country. The setting sun on the horizon beckoned them forward to the prosperity that they believed lay waiting for them in Rockafella.

rootlet 1.51 — what happened in Rockafella

As they got close to Rockafella, they saw a plume of black smoke over the town.

"Do you think something terrible has happened?" Pollyanna asked.

"Don't worry," reassured Gregor. "Even a small fire can create lots of smoke. "

When they reached the city limits, they discovered the smoke encapsulating Rockafella was from trucks and construction equipment. The preliminary steel framework of skyscrapers stood where quaint country houses once lined shaded streets. Hollering men in hardhats attacked the earth with roaring machines. Dust flew from trucks as they maneuvered around piles of debris like army tanks in a destroyed desert city. Pollyanna and Gregor were stunned when they found a real estate office where Uncle Sam's house once stood. In place of Sam's mailbox was a sign that read: Mr. Kappy L. Ism, Rental Expert.

Gregor pulled the car into the large parking lot that was once Sam's lawn. Pollyanna and Gregor could clearly see the office on the first floor through the large windows. The only furniture in the office was a shiny desk and three chairs. A young man in a nice-looking suit was sitting behind the desk in one of the chairs. The other two chairs were in front of the desk. Pollyanna and Gregor entered the office and looked at the man with bewilderment. He was leaning backward in his chair smoking a gigantic cigar with a cell phone wedged between his shoulder and cheek. The sign at the head of the desk read: Mr. Kappy L. Ism. Also on the desk were an ashtray, a humidor, a goldfish bowl, a miniature model gas pump, and a percolator with a bell-shaped knob.

"Please connect me to the office of Mr. Arthur F. Icial right away," said the man into the phone. "No, I can't wait, this is very important. I must speak to Mr. Icial immediately." The man covered the phone's mouthpiece and said to Gregor, "I'll be with you in just a moment. Hey Arthur. How are you doing? Listen, I just bought a top-of-the-line set of golf clubs. What are you doing—"

"Where is my Uncle Sam," Pollyanna interrupted, "and what has happened to this town?" The man froze for a second and stared at Pollyanna.

"Arthur can I call you back? I got a little situation here. Okay, thanks." The man hung up the phone and inhaled deeply on his cigar. "Hi, I'm Kappy," gushed the man. Kappy thrust his hand over the desk and vice gripped Gregor's hand. "What can I do for you folks?" Thick white smoke billowed from his mouth, which he was straining into an exaggerated smile.

"What has happened here?" asked Pollyanna. "Where is my Uncle Sam, and what has happened to his house?"

Kappy put his cigar in the ashtray, popped out of his seat, and approached Pollyanna.

"Oh," he said, "you're Sam's niece, Pollyanna. When he was selling me the house, he spoke of you with great fondness." Kappy turned toward Gregor and clasped his hand again. "You must be Gregor. Sam mentioned you as well. He did tell you folks that he sold the house, didn't he?" asked Kappy.

"If he was thinking of selling the house he would have told me," Pollyanna said.

"Oh wow, looks like there has been some major miscommunication here. Why don't you folks have a seat? We'll get this matter cleared up right away." Kappy stooped slightly and gestured towards the chairs with an elegant sweep of his arm. Pollyanna and Gregor sat down and looked expectantly at Kappy. Kappy pointed at his fishbowl and said, "What do you think of my fishbowl?" Kappy's fishbowl consisted of a plastic fish encased within a solid hunk of clear plastic. "My friend Arty's company designed that fishbowl," Kappy said proudly. Kappy handed a business card to Gregor, which read: <u>Mr. Arthur F. Icial, Presiding President, REALREPLICAS.COM. Our world-renowned staff of craftsmen duplicates every aspect of a product EXCEPT the high cost.</u>

Pollyanna snatched the card out of Gregor's hands. "Mr. Lism," she said. "I need to know what happened to my uncle."

"Yes, well of course," said Kappy. "Let me personally assure you that your uncle is very happy."

"Well where is he?" asked Pollyanna. Kappy plucked the bell-shaped knob off the percolator.

"Say, would you folks like a drink? I know I could use one."

"Listen, I just want to know where my uncle—" ding a ling a ling! Mr. Lism shook the knob violently. A back door opened and a foreign-looking woman trudged into the office. The woman went to Mr. Lism's side and froze like a statue. She had a weathered face that was devoid of emotion.

"What can I do for you Mr. Lism?" she said in a monotone voice.

"Slavetia, I'd like you to meet Gregor and Pollyanna. Gregor and Pollyanna this is my office maid Mrs. Slavetia Pavlov." Kappy looked up at Slavetia with his strained grin and said, "Could you be a doll and bring us three cups of milk and honey?"

"No! I don't want any milk and honey!" Pollyanna yelled. "I just want to know where my uncle is!" Slavetia stopped and looked at Mr. Lism for further instruction.

"Never mind the milk and honey," Kappy whispered to Slavetia. "Just bring me one of my lotus cigars." Slavetia bowed slightly and whisked herself out of the office.

"Mr. Lism!" Pollyanna growled. "Why do you avoid telling us where my Uncle Sam is?"

"I am trying to help you," Kappy said politely.

"If you want to help me, stop playing games and tell me where he is this minute."

"I don't know where he is."

Pollyanna blew out a puff of exasperation and said, "If you don't know where he is, why did you tell us he was very happy?"

"Well because I'm an optimist at heart and I feel certain that wherever your uncle is, he is happy."

"You mean you don't know how he is doing either?"

"I paid your uncle two million dollars for his house. He looked happy to me when he took the money."

Gregor snapped out of his prolonged silence and slammed his fist down on the desk. "That's absurd!" he barked. "This lot is worth two hundred thousand dollars at the most."

"Actually," replied Kappy, "I just sold the house to someone this morning for ten million dollars."

"Ten million dollars!" said Gregor. "Why would someone spend ten million dollars on a house like this?"

Kappy sprung from his chair like a jack-in-the-box. "The Black Gold coffee shop is why!" he projected with theatrical flair.

Pollyanna and Gregor became very quiet. "You mean that little coffee shop in town?" asked Pollyanna.

"Yes," said Kappy. "The first customers discovered that Black Gold's coffee provided much more energy than any beverage has before. A few corporations learned of Black Gold's coffee and immediately rushed to move their offices to this town. They figured the consumption of high-energy coffee would greatly enhance the productivity of their employees. When I heard about what was happening, I knew the price of real estate in Rockafella was going to explode. I came to this town and bought as much real estate as I could."

Slavetia came back into the office and handed Kappy a yellow cigar. Kappy took the cigar and sat back down in his chair. He held the cigar horizontally in his two hands for Gregor and

Pollyanna to view and said, "I own the company that produced this cigar. My cigar company is located on the island of Lotophagi, which is the only place in the world where the lotus fruit grows. The yellow on this cigar is the skin from the lotus fruit, which we use to wrap our tobacco. My company is the only one to produce cigars with authentic lotus fruit skin."

"Wonderful. Are you going to help us find Sam with a yellow cigar?" asked Gregor.

Instead of responding to Gregor's comment, Kappy clicked a little lever on the side of the miniature gas pump. A small steady flame shot out from the pump's nozzle. Kappy clutched the rubber just under the nozzle like a man handling a poisonous snake. He lit the cigar and began puffing away. Purple smoke streamed from his mouth. The streams formed large round plumes that bunched together like a cluster of grapes.

Kappy leaned forward and blew smoke at Gregor. The smoke had a wine-like smell, and made Gregor feel very relaxed. "I can't help you find Sam," Kappy said. "However, I can help you forget about Sam. All who breathe the smoke from this cigar forget everything that troubles them."

Gregor smiled at Kappy and asked softly, "What happens when the effect wears off?"

"Soon you will not worry about what happens when the effect wears off," Kappy replied. He exhaled another purple plume and began tapping the desk with his index finger. Blackness engulfed Gregor like the amniotic fluid that cushions the fetus in the womb. The sound of Kappy's finger tapping the desk was as comforting as a mother's heartbeat. Gregor's worries dissipated, and his consciousness receded like a wave flowing back into the ocean after breaking. Soon Gregor was in the deep slumber of the unborn.

rootlet 1.52 — the effects of the lotus cigar

A horrifying scream jolted Gregor from his slumber. He opened his eyes and found he was sitting alone in a gray rocky basin. A merciless sun beat down on the landscape with harsh rays of light. On the other side of the basin was a giant machine that looked like a great yellow bird. The machine had a long neck with a pointed head at the end that bobbed up and down like a bird pecking for worms.

Suddenly, there was another horrifying scream behind Gregor. He whirled around and saw a goat standing by the upturned roots of a massive fallen tree. The goat had a purple beard and was cross-eyed. He grinned at Gregor and jumped into the pit that the tree's roots had left behind, when they had ripped out of the ground. The goat put his front hooves on the edge of the pit and catapulted his back hooves over his head. He balanced upside down at the pit's edge for a moment before slamming his hooves back into the pit. The slamming hooves kicked up a cloud of dust that engulfed both goat and pit from Gregor's sight. Inside the dust cloud, the sound of the goat's wild laughter boomed like thunder.

After a short while, the goat grew silent. The dust dissipated and lying next to the pit was a four-foot-long coffee thermos that had inexplicably appeared. The goat was standing on top of the thermos glaring at the pecking machine.

He took a deep breath and unleashed a long steady scream across the basin. The pecking machine creaked and fell over with a deep thud that shook the ground. The goat stopped screaming and jumped nimbly to the ground. He looked at Gregor, smiled, and crawled inside the thermos.

Gregor walked over to the thermos and looked inside. The goat was gone. Instead, Gregor found swarms of ants lining the inner walls of the thermos in a writhing blanket. On the ground by the thermos's opening was a sticky dark patch where the coffee had spilled and dehydrated. Millions of ants were stuck in the patch slowly dying in the viscous mire. The dying ants formed a bridge that the other ants used to march in and out of the thermos.

The ants that left the thermos crossed over the coffee patch and went to their colony, which was in the pit by the fallen tree. Gregor looked in the pit and beheld thousands of ants laboring industriously to fix the damage that the goat had caused. Gregor watched as hundreds of ants worked in unison to drag one big clod out of the colony. They had the clod almost out of the pit when the sand under them gave way, and the clod tumbled back down.

rootlet 1.53 — Gregor follows his instincts through the consciousness of chaos

Suddenly, the sound of thunder rumbled across the basin. Streams of black smoke drifted over the hills from the west, and a coffee-scented breeze blew through the basin. The scent stimulated an urge in Gregor, which overrode all else in his mind. His sense of self-awareness evaporated into the singular focus of heading west.

He drifted westward across the basin like a jellyfish drifting on a current across the ocean. His state of unconscious focus did not waver until several hours later when he came to the end of the basin and the flat terrain began to incline. He became aware that he was standing at the entrance of a path that wound up a mountain. Gregor smelled the coffee again and his singular focus of heading west returned. He began to climb up the hill with the blind intensity of a fish swimming upstream to spawn.

Gregor's attention only wavered several hours later when he got to the top of the hill and the inclining terrain began to flatten. He became aware that nestled between the mountains in front of him was a huge metallic cylinder. The cylinder was in the center of a huge basin and he could just make out a thread-like pattern that branched outward from the cylinder's base like roots from a tree.

Gregor descended towards the cylinder with the unconscious focus of a hatchling salmon heading toward the sea. His consciousness returned when the mountain was behind him and he was at the edge of the basin. The pit was about a mile in circumference and several hundred feet deep. He saw that the thread-like pattern spreading from the base of the cylinder was actually a network of pipes. In the outer portion of the crater, several gigantic cranes were scooping up the soil like metal earth-eating dinosaurs. The largest of the beasts began to extend his metal neck out of the pit and over Gregor's head.

Suddenly, the crane's scoop swung open, and out fell the goat with the purple beard. The goat landed nimbly on his feet and trotted away from the pit towards a large crack in the sheer side of a cliff. When he got to the crack, he looked over his shoulder and smiled at Gregor. Then he squeezed into the crack and vanished.

Gregor walked over to the cliff and poked his head inside the crack. The narrow slit expanded into a wide stone passageway about twenty feet long. At the end of the passageway, the goat was sticking his head out from around a bend and grinning at Gregor. Gregor turned his body sideways and squeezed into the crack after the goat. When he entered the passageway, the goat laughed and pulled his head out of sight. Gregor turned the corner and entered a rounded passageway with perfectly smooth walls. The distant side of the passageway tapered like a cone into a small round hole through which sunlight streamed. Gregor walked forward until the shrinking passageway forced him to crawl. As he neared the end of the tunnel, he had to continue on his stomach and wriggle forward.

When he was just a few feet shy of the hole, the tunnel became too tight for him to progress. He was about to wriggle backwards, when the sunlight streaming through the hole brightened. The walls of the tunnel softened and became warm. Suddenly, the tunnel began to rhythmically contract and push Gregor forward. The contractions climaxed into a steady crushing constriction that squeezed all the air from him. Unable to breathe,

Gregor slipped into unconsciousness. Then, the constrictions ended, and cool clean air rushed into his lungs.

rootlet 1.54 — Gregor meets Bacchus

Gregor regained consciousness and saw a blur of green. As more air entered his body, his senses returned. He was lying on the ground and his chest was heaving. In front of his face was a thick patch of grass. Gregor stood up and put his hands to his knees. For several minutes, he remained in that position gasping for air. After he caught his breath, he stood up and looked around. He was in a tiny valley sunken deep into a mountain range. Nowhere on the surrounding cliffs, could he find the hole whence he came. In the center of the valley stood a giant tree that grew far above the surrounding cliffs and shaded the entire area. A man in a purple robe, who was smoking a pipe, stepped out from behind the tree and beckoned Gregor to approach.

As Gregor approached, the man gently exhaled smoke as white as clouds. When Gregor got to the tree, the man said nothing and continued to exhale plumes of white. After a couple of minutes, Gregor finally said, "My name is Gregor. What is your name?"

"My name is Bacchus," said the man.

Bacchus looked like refreshing coolness and restful nights. His dark eyes radiated warmth and sparkled like a summer evening sky, and his velvety hair curled like the slow turning vortices in a gentle stream. He inhaled on his pipe and blew out a plume of white smoke tinged with purple and redolent of wine. The plume unfurled into flickering, flame-like wisps that twirled playfully in the air.

"Where are you from?" he asked Gregor.

"I am from the edge of a great basin in which a herd of giant metal beasts were eating soil."

"How did you get to this valley?"

"One of the beasts stretched his neck out of the pit and regurgitated a goat with a purple beard. I followed that goat into a passageway that led to this courtyard."

"You must have inhaled the smoke from a lotus cigar. The purple-bearded goat only appears to those rare few who have the enormous will necessary to overcome the lotus smoke."

"I never inhaled any smoke," replied Gregor.

"You simply don't remember," said Bacchus. "All who inhale the smoke from the lotus cigar become very susceptible to routine. When these individuals engage in routine; their minds narrow, until they can focus only on the routine. Since none of their thoughts meander to their past or future, the lotus smokers lose their sense of self. They become like ants that interact with the world through instinct alone. Even the very routine of putting one's foot in front of the other while walking can cause the lotus smoker's consciousness to harden into instinct. Only when their environment drastically changes around them and obviates their routine do their instincts liquefy back into consciousness. Unfortunately, the main side effect of the lotus smoke is that the smokers lose all their memory save their name. When they reawaken, they accept without question the world they perceive as a permanent reality. Only when they have retained consciousness long enough to witness the world change do they develop a sense of past."

Bacchus paused for a moment and took a few reflective puffs on his pipe. "The memory that the re-awakened accumulates is fleeting," he said. "As soon as they engage in any routine or repetitious activity, their mind re-solidifies back into the focus of instinct and their memories evaporate away again."

Bacchus again began puffing on his pipe and exhaled purple smoke that smelled distinctly of wine. Gregor slowly relaxed and sat down with his back against the tree. In the sky, the clouds flowed eastward in turbulent whorls, while the sun drifted calmly towards the west. When the sun began to dip under the cover of the western horizon, the smoke coming from Bacchus' pipe darkened into the deep purple of the ripest grapes. Bacchus exhaled one final plume and finished his pipe just as the top of the sun dipped below sight.

He turned to Gregor and said, "Come, I will show you where you can stay." Gregor followed Bacchus to a cave on the side of the valley. At the cave's entrance, a single torch flickering from a holder provided the only light. Bacchus took the torch out of the holder and led Gregor into the cave. They went down a flight of stone stairs and entered a stone chamber that had a small root protruding from the cave's ceiling. When Bacchus saw the root he said, "That root is from the tree in the valley. Only a tree looking for truth would send a root this deep. From this root, I will carve you a pipe that may help counteract the lotus smoke."

rootlet 1.55 — Gregor remembers bits and pieces

The sun glowed deep orange, like flames shadowing the heart of a fire. As Gregor inhaled on his pipe and blew another plume of smoke into the air, he continued to reflect on Bacchus and his last few days at Black Gold. How he had come to work at Black Gold continued to evade his memory. He watched the smoke from the pipe swirl into a column-like shape. Smoke attenuated from the column's base into thin root-like wisps. As Gregor watched the smoke-roots drift towards the ground and dissolve, he suddenly remembered the sequence of events from when he first saw the pit to just before when Bacchus stepped out from behind the tree. Gregor surmised that the pit he remembered seeing was the Black Gold coffee station in the early stages of its construction. The tunnel that he used to walk through every day to get to work seemed to be in the same location as the crack that had led him to the valley. Gregor could not apprehend how the tunnel, the dome over the valley, and the coffee station came into existence without him noticing.

    Gregor finished smoking his pipe just as the sun settled beneath the hills, and headed back to his cave. At the top of the stone stairs, was a string that hung from the ceiling. He pulled the string, and a dim yellow light struggled against the darkness below like a dying ember. Gregor stood stunned, as he realized that the cave had acquired electricity since Bacchus had first showed him the root.

    When Gregor reached the bottom of the stairs, he stopped and looked at the huge root that grew from the ceiling. Suddenly he remembered the snippet of time from when Bacchus led him into the cave, to when he first saw the root. The root had since grown as thick as a tree and extended down from the ceiling and through a deep crack in the stone floor. Gregor could not remember ever noticing the root growing. Indeed, Gregor realized he could remember nothing that had occurred before he lost his job at Black Gold except his memories of Bacchus. He did not know how his cave had been wired for electricity, or how he had obtained personal belongings.

Gregor walked over a thick wooden plank that spanned the crack and entered the cave's main body. In the cave's center, a large square plank rested upon two wooden horses and formed a makeshift table. The cigar Ludwig had given him was in the center of the table. Near the wall furthest from the base of the stairs, a decaying orange recliner was unfolded into a bed. The rusting metal frame bent severely and touched the floor with one corner. On the sloping frame, dirty blankets and papers bunched together into a semi-concave mass that resembled a giant rat's nest.

Around the bed was a tremendous pile of clothes that spread amorphously outward like an oil spill. Intermingled with the clothes were metal gears, pipes, and bits of wire. The metal pieces were the remnants of Gregor's coffecation machine that used to sit on the makeshift table. Gregor had never tried to use the machine until the day after he lost his job. When he put the briquettes into the grinding chamber and pressed the on switch, the machine made an ugly grating sound and began to smoke. Gregor figured that something had caught in one of the gears and that he could easily fix the machine. When he took off the machine's casing, however, the incomprehensible mass of gears underneath unnerved him.

He decided to carefully take apart the machine piece by piece until he found the cause of the problem. Many hours later, he triumphantly found two gears that had come loose and were not properly interlocking. He tightened a few screws, and the gears shifted snugly together.

Unfortunately, reassembling the machine proved far more difficult then dissembling the machine had been. He became confused as to what the machine's original configuration was and incorrectly reconnected many of the pieces. The more he tried to fix his mistakes the more the machine came undone. After two weeks, he had unwittingly disassembled the entire machine and strewn the parts across the floor.

Gregor sat down on his bed rested his chin in his hand and tried again to remember the missing sequences of his life. Although he had just smoked his pipe, he still had an urge to smoke more. He lit a match and took the cigar Ludwig had given him off the table. As soon as Gregor touched the flame to the cigar, the cigar made a tremendous farting sound. A blast of foul air rushed from the cigar's end and filled the cave with the overwhelming stench of rotten eggs. Gregor dropped the cigar onto the floor, and jerked away. An orifice opened up at the end of the cigar, and a procession of feces came out like a never-ending train emerging from a tunnel. In only a few seconds, the cigar produced a deep pile of dung. Gregor regained his senses and with a well-placed kick sent the defecating cigar tumbling towards the crack. The cigar emitted a staccato fart with each bounce off the floor and then tumbled into the crack with resonating flatulence.

    Gregor stood still until the fart's echo subsided into silence. He crept cautiously towards the crack and peered over the edge. Suddenly a cane snapped out from the crack like a frog's tongue striking at an insect. In a blink, the cane hooked Gregor around the neck and pulled him into the crack.

OFFSHOOT TWO

ENTROPIS

ROOT 2.1 — GREGOR MEETS ENTROPIS

When he regained his senses, Gregor discovered that he was stuck up to his shoulders in manure. Above his head were the asses of two horses. Gregor tried to free himself from the manure and could not. "Is anybody here, I need some help!" he yelled.

"Topsy and Turvy backward Ho," responded a voice. The horses neighed and reared their asses. Gregor saw the hooves coming down and closed his eyes. When he opened his eyes, the horses were somewhere behind him. "Topsy and Turvy backward Ho," repeated the voice. Soon the sound of the voice subsided into silence somewhere behind Gregor. Then Gregor heard the voice resonating faintly from somewhere in front of him. The voice began to gradually increase in loudness, until the horses' asses emerged from the darkness in front of Gregor.

In front of the horse's heads was a cart, in which rode a long shadowy figure. The horses moved in disunion with each other, and the cart in front of them jerked forward in fits and snatches. The shadowy figure flickered with each jerk as if he was a black flame feasting on the wasted energy. The horses continued haltingly until their asses were in the same place above Gregor's head as when they had begun their backward excursion.

"Topsy and Turvy," said the voice, "Dissipate away." The horses reared their asses and expelled long farts, which resonated like rolling thunder. A noxious stream of smoke effused from their anuses and blinded Gregor. When the rolling fart stopped, the smoke began to clear.

Gregor saw cloven hoofs sunk into the dung only inches from his face. A clawed hand grabbed Gregor by the hair, plucked him out of the dung like a vegetable and held him high off the ground. As he dangled from his hair, Gregor looked into the strangest face he had ever seen.

The figure had a goat's head covered with boils that oozed with pus. The weight of the boils pulled his flesh down and exposed the area underneath his eyes like two raw wounds. His eyes moved in the most mysterious manner. His right eye rolled rightward at a rather rapid rate, while his left eye looped leftward at a somewhat slower pace. The middle of his mouth crimped; yet, the corners were open wide. His mouth looked like an hourglass tipped over to a side. From his mouth's corners came smoke in snuffs and puffs that unfurled into the air like wispy mustache tufts. "Who grows from my fertile soil?" asked the figure. Gregor was too shocked to answer. The goat man began to shake Gregor in small violent bursts as if he were shaking dirt from a freshly picked carrot. After he had shaken Gregor relatively clean, he put him down. The goat man stood in front of Gregor with his clawed hands resting on a walking cane. He wore a long black cloak that covered all of his body except his head, hands, and hooves. Half of the cloak was tattered and covered in dung, while the other half seemed to be in perfect condition.

    Gregor looked around and saw that he was in a vast subterranean wasteland of smoldering dung. There was a dirt sky overhead, from which giant roots grew all the way down and into the dung. Throughout the upside-down forest were piles of dung that in spots glowed orange like cooling lava. Tendrils of smoke wafted from the piles and drifted aimlessly through the roots like bored ghosts.

"Who are you?" Gregor asked. The goat creature opened his mouth, and smoke billowed out as he spoke in a disharmonious strained voice.

"I am Entropis, Demon of Dung,

Master of smoke that burns in your lung,

Lord of all that's dead and decaying,

Bringer of wrinkles and hair that is graying.

My name whispers from wishers of change,

From those who are bored or completely deranged.

I send them tornadoes, earthquakes, and fire.

I reduce their existence to rubble and mire.

Whenever lives have reached their worst,

Where there is oppression and animals curse,

My power is what these desperate desire;

To fight the system against which they conspire.

I help them all on one condition;

New order built from their volition.

If they cannot endure this pain,

Upon their soul, I make my claim."

ROOT 2.2 —THE CANE OF CHAOS

"Behold my Cane of Chaos!" shrieked Entropis. Entropis held the cane in front of Gregor. The staff was comprised of two intertwining snakes. As the staff curved to form the handle, the two snakes merged to form one head with three eyes. "These two snakes are the two orders of chaos."

"The two orders of chaos?" said Gregor. "What do you mean?"

Entropis hurled his staff like a spear into the dung. "Cane of Chaos!" he shrieked. "Show me your order." The snakes in the cane came alive and collapsed to the dung in a writhing tangled pile. They untangled and slithered through the dung until they reached the cloven hoofs of Entropis. One snake slithered clockwise up his left leg, and the other slithered counter-clockwise up his right leg. The snakes disappeared inside Entropis' cloak and then re-emerged at the collar of his head. They circled once around his neck in opposite directions before re-entering his cloak again. Entropis held his arms stiffly in front of him with his palms facing forward. The snakes emerged from both sleeves simultaneously and began to slither down his arms. When they had almost passed through his clawed hands, Entropis clenched them by the tip of their tails and cracked them in the air like whips. The snakes became frozen with their heads bent at right angles from their straight bodies and their mouths wide open.

Entropis held the snakes in either claw and said, "These are the pipes of Familiar and Familiar-Not. Whoever can smoke them both at once gets wisdom on the spot. Familiar is fashionable with the practical and mundane, while Familiar-Not is smoked amongst the creative and insane."

Entropis reached into his pocket and took out some dried dung, which he put in the mouth of Familiar-Not. He then used a glowing ember of dung from the ground to light the pipe. As he puffed on the pipe, the dung in the bowl turned bright orange. Entropis took a mighty breath and exhaled great eddies of smoke from the corners of his hour-glass-mouth. The smoke eddies expanded into a plume, which engulfed Gregor. Within the plume, a rectangular space the size of a large room formed around him. The side farthest from Gregor dissolved away and revealed an empty gray landscape. Gregor saw a quiescent gray ocean with gray mountains in the background. Suddenly, lightning flashed over the mountains and struck the ocean like a lion's paw. Where the lightning had struck, the water boiled and waves formed that traveled outward in ever widening rings. At the same time, large bubbles began to form within the rectangular space. A large bubble slowly swelled up in front of Gregor and suddenly burst into multicolored smoke and sparks. When the smoke cleared, there was a counter where the bubble had been. On top of the counter smaller bubbles were rapidly forming and bursting like a series of firecrackers. A cash register and a pastry case replete with pastries sprung into existence on top of the counter.

  Throughout the space were other bubbles that were bursting into tables and chairs. Above, bubbles burst into lights and a ventilation duct. On the vertical sides of the space, shelves formed that were full of grinders, brewers, and other coffee related equipment. After a short spell, the bubbles stopped bursting. The rectangular space had become a coffee shop save for the far wall, which was still missing.

  Gregor was standing behind the counter at a register. A wave from the gray ocean broke on the near shore and washed all the way to the counter before receding. The receding wave left behind a creature with a man's body and a lobster's head. The man-lobster was wearing a business suit and held a brief case in his right hand. Instead of a left hand, he had a giant claw. When he saw Gregor, he began snapping the claw menacingly in Gregor's face. "Is that cappuccino ready yet?" he asked. "I'm losing energy please hurry." Before Gregor could respond, he burst into a puff of smoke and vanished.

 Another wave just like the first flowed into the shop and left behind a woman with a squid's head and ten tentacles. She waved her tentacles wildly at Gregor and gurgled, "Is my mocha ready yet? Please hurry. I can't live without a mocha." Gregor tried his best to make her drink as fast as possible. He was just about to give her the mocha when she dissipated away in a puff of smoke.

 The next wave left behind an older man who wore a white lab coat over white pants and a white button-up shirt. He had a scorpion tail, which curved over his head and thrust threateningly at Gregor. "Give me a pound of coffee quick," demanded the scorpion man. "My children are in the car and they will die without coffee."

Before Gregor had time to respond, the scorpion man disappeared into thin air.

Waves kept washing one coffee-craving creature after another into the coffee shop. Although Gregor did his best to serve them, they always dissipated away before he could get them their coffee.

Suddenly, the coffee shop exploded and dissolved away. Gregor was back in the upside-down forest. Entropis stood in front of him cleaning the stem of Familiar-Not with a long wiggling centipede. When he was finished, he flung the centipede into the air. The centipede burst into smoke and interfused with the smoke of the dung.

"Entropis," Gregor asked, "What do you mean to say that there is order in what I have just seen?"

Entropis replied in a voice that varied wildly in pitch:

"What I can say with certainty

About Unfamiliarity

Is that every creature past

Will be as unfamiliar as the last.

Try Familiarity

And you will see with clarity

That there is some disparity

Between these scaly pipes."

Entropis took the pipe with the repeating patterns and exhaled another plume of smoke. A rectangular space that overlooked a gray ocean formed around Gregor just like before. The space began to bubble in the exact manner that the previous one had. When the bubbling was finished, Gregor was again standing at a register behind a counter. A wave from the ocean broke along the shore and washed all the way to the counter before receding. Instead of a man-lobster, however, the receding wave left behind a regular human man. The man was wearing a suit and was carrying a brief case. "Is that cappuccino ready yet?" he asked. "I'm beginning to fade here, please hurry." Before Gregor could respond, he burst into a puff of smoke and vanished. Each subsequent wave washed in another coffee-craving person. Gregor tried his best to serve the customers. Unfortunately, they always dissipated away before he could help them.

Suddenly, the coffee shop exploded and dissolved away. Gregor was back in the upside-down forest. Entropis stood in front of him cleaning the stem of familiar with a long wiggling centipede. When he was finished, he flung the centipede into the air. The centipede burst into smoke and interfused with the smoke of the dung.

ROOT 2.3 — THE END OF GREGOR

"Entropis," Gregor said,

"Let me smoke Familiar and Familiar-Not together.

I'd like to see if smoking both makes me very clever."

"Gregor," said Entropis,

"For clever you already have the knack.

Balance is your need, and wisdom is your lack.

You cannot solve this problem with a little puffer.

The only cure for you is to struggle hard and suffer.

You will persist

To look for a truth that does not exist.

Anguish and pain will tear your ambition,

Until all that remains is your naked volition.

If your roots are deep enough,

You will re-grow healthy and tough.

The time has come for you to start your trip.

When you awake your memory will skip

All of this place's features.

Now dissipate away oh ignorant creature."

Entropis smoked both pipes at once and blew the smoke at Gregor. The smoke from the pipes engulfed Gregor and turned him into smoke. Ninety percent of Gregor dissipated away, while the other ten percent effused with the smoke from the pipes and formed a plume. Within the plume, the remaining essence of Gregor melded with the essences of the various animals that had excreted the dung. The plume entered an offshoot from one of the roots and flowed upward through a network of capillaries. The capillaries delivered the smoke up through the dirt sky and into the bowl of a giant pipe. The smoke then drifted out of the bowl and condensed into a hybrid creature.

The creature had the legs of an orangutan with hoofed feet. Two starkly mismatched arms hung from a torso that was scaly and lizard-like. The left arm was hairy, massive, and had an imposing bear-like claw. The right arm was fully human and had a hand with an opposable thumb. The top two-thirds of the creature's hybrid head was comprised of the inchoate heads of a boar, deer, and fox fused together. From their eyes to their scalps, the inchoate heads were distinctly separate from the hybrid head. Just below the creature's six eyes, the inchoate heads melded together to form a single nose. The nose had three nostrils and was a cauliflower like agglomeration of hundreds of fleshy buds. The three different furs from the inchoate heads mixed roughly together just below his six eyes and progressively commingled more evenly towards his nose. The commingling progression culminated in a thin horseshoe band of uniform brown fur that looped over the top of his nose. The creature's facial fur abruptly gave way to skin under his nose, for the small area encompassing his mouth and chin was fully human.

OFFSHOOT THREE

MANDELBROT

ROOT 3.1 — HECTIC NORDER MEETS MANDELBROT

The hybrid creature was standing in a large glen. In front of him was a massive yew tree. The tree was smoking a giant pipe, which was creating billows of smoke redolent of pine. The bowl of the pipe looked like a goat's head and the stem like two intertwining snakes. The tree took the pipe from his mouth and said, "Hello, I am Yew."

"Hello," said the creature. "I am Me."

"Do you have a name, Me?" asked Yew.

"No," said Me. "Do you?"

"No," said Yew.

Me thought for a moment and said, "If you give me a name, I will give you a name."

"I like that idea," said Yew. "Step forwards Me and let me look at you until I think of a name that appeals to me and fits to you." Me stepped forward, and Yew began to intently study him. After a moment Yew said, "Your name is Hectic Norder."

Hectic smiled and pointed at himself with his human index finger. "I am Hectic Norder!" he exclaimed.

"Yes," said Yew. "Now you give me a name."

Hectic stepped forward and looked reflectively at Yew. Rough, shaggy, bark splotched with lichen and moss covered all his face except his lips, which were smooth like the branches of a Japanese maple tree. His eyes were concavities that slowly secreted a resin that glowed orange like hot charcoal. Numerous globules fused loosely together to form his nose like the segments in a pile of cow dung. A well-groomed mustache of green and white needles connected to a long beard of vines that hung twenty feet off Yew's chin. Yew's gigantic roots reached from the base of Yew's trunk in all directions. His roots came out of the ground and plunged back in like a school of dolphins diving and plunging in an ocean of dirt. Some of his roots curved back towards him, climbed his trunk, and buried themselves into his bark.

Yew took a puff on his pipe and with a mischievous grin blew out a giant smoke ring. Hectic watched with amazement as the ring drifted over his head and then descended slowly around him. "How did you learn to form smoke rings?" asked Hectic. Yew began to roar with laughter. His gaping mouth was deep with a jagged interior like an ancient canyon. His huge tongue stuck out of his mouth, curved slightly upward and quivered with each burst of laughter. A filament of mucous stretched from the tip of his tongue to a huge swamp of slime with mushroom islands at the back of his mouth. "Your name is Mandelbrot!" yelled Hectic over the tree's laughing.

ROOT 3.2 — MANDELBROT REVEALS HIS PAST

Mandelbrot stopped laughing and his slug like tongue contracted back into his mouth. He smiled and said, "Since you have chosen a name that pleases me, I will show you how I learned to form such good smoke rings." Mandelbrot hesitated for a second and became very solemn. "The truth is," he said, "smoke rings are only one of the most basic shapes I form. I can create entire landscapes from smoke, which look real in every respect. Behold as I form images of my past and show you how I became the smoke master."

Mandelbrot's huge trunk expanded as he inhaled a mighty breath. A gale force wind rushed past Hectic and into Mandelbrot's canyon mouth. He held the storm inside of his swollen trunk for a moment and then blew into the stem of his pipe. The pipe emitted a tremendous roaring noise and the contents of the goat-head bowl glowed lava-orange. Columns of smoke rose from the bowl before attenuating and intertwining like vines. The smoke-vines drifted out into the space around Hectic like the tentacles of a jellyfish. The smoke tentacles branched into smaller tentacles until they formed a wicker-basket-like network around Hectic.

Through the slits of the wicker-smoke, Hectic saw Mandelbrot's beard of vines unravel. At the end of each vine was an undulating fin-shaped leaf. Mandelbrot maneuvered the school of leaves in a roughly spherical shape around the smoky basket that enveloped Hectic. He began to increase the movement of the leaves and roil the air. The currents in the air hit the smoky tendrils that formed the basket, and caused them to blend with each other into a sphere. Inside the sphere, Hectic watched the inner surface of the smoky enclosure take the appearance of a turbulent gray ocean. Waves of liquid smoke crashed into each other and formed gray eddies.

The sphere began to expand until Mandelbrot's face protruded through the section in front of Hectic. The section of the sphere behind and to the side of Hectic turned sky blue with puffy white clouds. The front section remained as a gray ocean with Mandelbrot's face jutting out like a small island. Hectic lost his sense of direction and felt as if he was hovering high in the sky.

Mandelbrot's face looked like an island in the ocean directly below him.

Mandelbrot spoke in a voice that resonated through the smoky sphere. He said, "Our minds are jellyfish and the world is a turbulent ocean. Many different kinds of waves crash about in the ocean that is our world. Over thousands of years, I have managed to learn about the waves of light. I have learned to control light through the medium of smoke and create what you see. I can direct the smoke to absorb certain light waves and reject others. In this way, I create images through hue, saturation, and brilliance. I will now alter the pattern, in which the leaves from my beard are moving. Notice the correlating change in the images you see."

Some of the waves in the horizon before Hectic rose out of the ocean and froze into gray mountains. Mandelbrot's face seamlessly shifted position to the horizon behind the mountains. The mountains began to draw closer to Hectic causing him to feel as if he was flying forward like a bird.

Hectic passed over the shoreline where the gray waters crashed upon jagged cliffs. Below him, he saw a swiftly flowing river rush through a fiord and empty into the ocean. Around the fiord, wispy clouds encircled the mountaintops like hair on the heads of ancient wise men. The image of the fiord seemed to grow bigger and Hectic felt as if he was dropping down into the fiord. He glided between the cliff walls of the fiord about fifty feet over the river like a hawk looking for a fish. Just below him, the angry river frothed with white water and slammed against the sides of the mountains with tremendous fury. The river pounded a protruding section of the mountain and broke loose a boulder. The boulder fell into the river and sent an explosion of water upward towards Hectic. Hectic tensed up as he anticipated the upsurge of water possibly knocking him out of flight. When the water droplets hit him, however; they turned into smoke and dissipated around him. With the smoke around him, Hectic remembered for a brief second that the images he saw were not real. He felt his feet against the ground and remembered that he was standing in the glen. As soon as the smoke from the droplets dissipated away, Mandelbrot's images again enthralled him.

    The fiord opened up into a valley, and the rushing water became a gentle stream. Hectic drifted just above the stream as if he was a little cloud. He drifted into a forest comprised of trees which, like Mandelbrot, had faces. Mandelbrot began to speak and his voice seemed to resonate from everywhere at once. His face was still off in the horizon as if a setting sun. He said, "This is the forest where I lived as a child." Mandelbrot pursed his lips and blew out a gentle stream of smoke that drifted down from the sky. The smoke infiltrated the forest and darkened everything. Hectic felt as if he was standing on the bottom of a murky pond. Then slowly the murk began to clear. In front of Hectic were a willow, a young sapling, and an oak tree.

    The oak's bark became extremely craggy around the mouth and chin to form a beard on the tree's masculine face. The oak was smoking a huge pipe with a thick round bowl. He furrowed his great brow into a look of intense concentration and blew out a spherical plume. Then, he put his pipe down by the base of his trunk and maneuvered his branches around the plume. When he had finished positioning his branches, he began quivering and sending small vibrations of air into the plume. The plume began to dissipate and form the images of numerous large lizard-like creatures. Soon the oak had created numerous dinosaurs, which the young sapling watched with intense fascination. The young sapling, who was between the oak and the willow, was watching the images with fascination. The sapling looked very adolescent with his thin trunk and gangly branches. He had a huge gnarled canopy of unkempt foliage, which he had to keep brushing from his eyes.

The willow had her foliage tied into a ponytail. She was busy knitting a sweater with two of her thin branches. On the front of the sweater, was a picture of a tree that's roots was clearly visible through the soil. The roots had the same shape as the branches, as if each was a reflection of the other. Nestled in the tree's roots was a mother ground hog nursing her young, and in the tree's branches, a mother squirrel was nursing her young.

The willow lifted the sweater over the young sapling and stretched the elastic base to fit over the sapling's canopy. The sapling's mop of a canopy popped through the turtleneck, and his skinny branches sprung out of the numerous holes that lined the sweater's side. He began straightening the sweater out with four branches and brushing leaves out of his eyes with his other branches.

Hectic was standing very close to the three trees and he kept wondering why they didn't see him. Then he would remember again that they were only an illusion that Mandelbrot was creating. Hectic looked down at the ground and realized that he could not see his body. Yet he could feel his hooves on the ground and his appendages hanging by his side. He moved his seemingly invisible hand and touched where his torso had been. He felt a thud and the space around the area of impact briefly turned into smoke. For a second, Hectic could see his hand floating in space and a small area of his lizard torso. Then the smoke re-coalesced and he was invisible again. He realized that Mandelbrot did not want the image of him in his landscape and had used the smoke to make him invisible. Hectic was like an imperceptible spirit whose only purpose was to observe.

Suddenly a rumbling emanated from above and the bowl of Mandelbrot's pipe jutted out of the clouds as if pushed through a canvas. He used his pipe to point at the young tree in the middle and said, "That was me when I was only 1200 years old. My parents called me Sprout. The weeping willow was my mother, and the oak tree was my father."

Mandelbrot took a deep breath and exhaled into his pipe. Smoke as black as ink, came out of the pipe and reached into the forest like the tentacles of a black squid. The blackness reached the three trees and swallowed them from Hectic's sight. The only light left came from the bowl of Mandelbrot's pipe and the tears of glowing sap that oozed from his eyes. The tears molassed onto his nose and hardened into amber. Mandelbrot spoke in a halting rumbling voice. He said, "Now I will show you that awful night when the ball of fire fell from the sky and destroyed my kin." Mandelbrot inhaled deeply on his pipe and blew smoke that quickly drifted from the light of his hardened tears into the surrounding darkness. At first, Hectic could see nothing. Then tiny flashes of light began blinking above him like fireflies. Some of the little white lights came together and formed a silvery quarter moon while the others formed stars. Hectic's view of the night sky then shifted downward as if the image was on a ball that someone was slowly rotating. The darkened images of the three trees sleeping under the night sky came into his view.

He saw Sprout wake up, stretch his branches, and yawn. Something in the sky caught Sprout's attention. Hectic looked up and saw a star burning brighter than the rest. The star began to quickly grow brighter. Hectic looked back over to the trees to see what they were doing. The light had woken up Willow who was reaching over Sprout and poking the sleeping Oak with her branch. By the time Oak had woken, the star had developed a tail and was burning brighter than the sun. Hectic saw Oak and Willow's face fill with terror as the light continued to intensify. They reached towards each other, interlocked their branches, and formed a spherical dome around Sprout.

  Mandelbrot's face burst through the smoky canvass. Instead of appearing in the sky, he appeared right before Hectic as if he was a giant floating head. Layers of glowing amber were congealing on his face, and he spoke in a voice that crackled like a fire trying to burn damp wood. "There were many days when I wished my parents had let me perish with them instead of saving my life," he said. He raised the pipe to his lips only to begin sobbing uncontrollably. Little rivulets of hot amber poured from his eyes and slid between the grooves of the amber that had cooled. After a moment he managed to contain his sobs long enough to exhale a deep breath into his pipe. A plume of smoke came forth that moved quickly towards Hectic like an angry swarm of bees. As the smoke engulfed him, he closed his eyes. When he opened his eyes, the smoke had congealed around him in the form of Sprout's body. He could see branches extending from him as if he was the young tree.

All around him was the protective dome of Oak and Willow's intertwining branches. Their faces seemed interwoven into the top of the sphere like a design embroidered into a quilt. They were both crying tears of amber, which oozed down the dome's inner walls and illuminated their faces.

There was a blinding flash of light followed by darkness. All Hectic could see was the bowl of Mandelbrot's pipe glowing dimly above him. Hectic heard Mandelbrot groan and saw the bowl of the pipe turn upside down. The ambers of the pipe scattered through the darkness and provided Hellish illumination. The once idyllic valley had become a wasteland of darkness, smoke, and smoldering ash.

Oak lay dead on his side. All his glorious foliage had incinerated and his massive trunk was burning. A stream of hot sap dribbled from his mouth and boiled on the ground. Willow was still alive but lay uprooted near Oak. The flames had consumed most of her foliage and charred her trunk. As she gasped for breath, she reached through the sooty air to where Oak lay. When she touched Oak's trunk, her branch caught on fire. She let the fire consume her, and her branch crumbled into ash and mixed with the ash from Oak.

Hectic saw the gangly branches reach from him as if he was Sprout reaching for his mother. She was too far away for the branches to reach her. With one of her remaining branches, Willow reached out to Sprout. The twigs from their branches intertwined like fingers from a pair of hands. She smiled tenderly towards Hectic even as she lay smoldering. Suddenly her face contorted and became still. The branch she was reaching out with broke from her trunk and fell to the burning ground. As the flames ate away at her body, she took her last breath and died.

The entire forest of trees was on fire. The rapacious flames shot up the trunks of terrified trees, licked their faces, and turned them black. The trees contorted in pain as the flames ate their cheeks of bark away. Soon there was nothing more of the forest except blackened trunks smoldering in a land of soot.

Mandelbrot's face swelled bigger. Sparks flew from his pipe and the amber under his eyes glowed brighter than ever. "Since that night I have been alone for millions of years!" he bellowed. "All the trees in the forest died except for me. The sunny valley where I was born stayed the gloomy wasteland that you see now for a millennia. I had to live alone in a world of soot and decay, with nothing to keep me company but my father's pipe."

Mandelbrot suddenly seemed old and gray. The amber on his face had stopped glowing and his rage had fizzled into weary sorrow. He inhaled very slowly and sent a steady weak breeze through his pipe. Thin gray sheets of smoke wafted down upon the dark valley and induced slight changes in the images. The black soot lightened into a dark gray and some of the charred branches on the trees vanished. Hectic saw Sprout in front of him and realized that Mandelbrot had altered his perspective of the landscape. Sprout had grown taller and skinnier. His branches were long and lanky and the bark around his face had developed red splotches. In his twigs, he held his father's pipe. "I wanted to learn how to create images from smoke even better then my father," Mandelbrot explained from above. "I wanted to use his pipe to recreate the sunny valley from my childhood and bring my parents back. I kept the ash of my parents in the hollow that the fireball had burned into the heart of my trunk." Mandelbrot hesitated for a moment. "I was only a stupid child," he sighed. "I had nobody to teach me. Every day I would smoke their ash and try to blow plumes in their image."

The landscape began to blur and then refocused into a slightly different landscape. Sprout was a little taller now, but not quite as gangly as before. Hectic watched as Sprout took a curved piece of bark and scooped some ash from the ground. He carefully bent the bark and created a crease, which he used to tap the ash into the pipe. "Although I tried my best to recreate my parent's image in the smoke, I could not. I still had much to learn about the art of smoke imagery." Sprout remained motionless for a moment and appeared to be deeply concentrating. He finally took a deep breath and exhaled into the pipe. His lips seemed inflexible and did not form a tight seal around the stem. As Sprout continued to blow, clear sap escaped from the corner of his mouth and dribbled down his chin. He began to flail his gangly arms at the dust and smoke that spurted from the bowl. His movements were clumsy and uncontrolled. He accidentally whipped himself in the face causing a small wound to open up under his eye. As the sap from his cut trickled down his cheek, Sprout furrowed his brow and tried even harder. His vines whipped faster and more frenetically. Despite his best efforts, the smoke began to dissipate. Soon the smoke was all gone and Sprout had hopelessly tangled his vines together in a huge knot. Sprout dropped his pipe onto the ashy ground, his trunk slumped, and all his branches hung loosely at his side. His gawky splotched face began to quiver and amber tears oozed from his eyes as he began to sob.

When Mandelbrot next spoke, the sky around him had become blue. His anger had left and he spoke in a hopeful tone. He said, "After another few thousand years, the sky and river began to clear." Mandelbrot exhaled a vigorous zephyr of wind into the pipe. Blue and green smoke effused from the pipe and came down upon Hectic. The smoke was too thick for him to see through. All he could see was swirls of blue and green.

As the smoke began to differentiate into blurry images, Mandelbrot began to speak. "When I was about twenty-eight hundred years old, the soot and ash had lifted from the valley."

Hectic looked around and saw that a thick carpet of grass and low-lying vegetation covered the valley. Sprout had grown considerably over the last thousand years. The red blotches were gone from his face and the unruly mop of leaves had become a handsome canopy. He sported a thick beard of green leafy vines. His trunk had grown much thicker than before and had become three times as long. Sprout, the young adult, held his father's pipe in his branches with confidence. He put the pipe to his mouth and formed a tight seal around the stem with his lips. Thick plumes of smoke puffed from the pipe's bowl like amorphous lumps of clay ready for shaping. Sprout furrowed his brow and with great dexterity began to unravel the vines of his beard. He stretched the vines out around the plume and began to quiver the leaves. The plumes began to shape into the rough but distinct images of his parents Willow and Oak. Sprout furrowed his brow even deeper and appeared to be struggling to refine his parent's image. Despite his best efforts, he could only keep the images stable for a few seconds. Nevertheless, Sprout's eyes had a flash of hope in them. Instead of crying as he had a thousand years before, Sprout gamely put the pipe to his lips and tried again.

Mandelbrot spoke from above. "After a few thousand more years of practice, I was able to form any image that I wanted. Alas, my success did not bring me the happiness I had expected." Mandelbrot blew out a plume of green smoke speckled with red, brown, and sparks of light. The smoke drifted down from the sky and blurred Hectic's vision, before coalescing into another image of the valley. The green valley had matured into a forest. Unlike the old forest however, the trees were of the ordinary variety and did not appear conscious like Mandelbrot. In the center of the valley was Sprout. Sprout took his pipe and blew a perfect sphere of smoke. He quickly unraveled his beard and with great ease formed the perfect likeness of his parents.

"Alas," said Mandelbrot from above, "although the images I created looked real, they were not living companions." Hectic watched as Sprout reached for his parents. When he touched their images, they immediately dissipated back into smoke. Sprout's smile also dissipated as the wisps of smoke from his parent's images drifted through his branches.

ROOT 3.3 — MANDELBROT'S STRUGGLE TO MASTER NATURE

Mandelbrot put the pipe to his lips and inhaled a mighty breath. The valley turned into smoke and streamed into the bowl of Mandelbrot's pipe. Hectic was back in the glen with Mandelbrot. On the ground, Hectic saw the shadow of his orangutan legs and realized that Mandelbrot was no longer maintaining the smoky illusion. Hectic looked down and saw his mismatched arms hanging from his lizard torso.

In front of him, he could again see Mandelbrot's entire trunk. The vines that Mandelbrot had used to manipulate the smoke had raveled back into the thick long beard that hung from his chin. Mandelbrot raised the pipe to his lips and blew out a plume of smoke. As the smoke unfurled, he began to stroke his leafy beard with his twig-like fingers.

"Despite all my efforts, I was still all alone," he said softly. "I had no one to talk to or play with. I wanted to create another tree that would talk to me, or at least create another creature that would keep me company. I decided to study the world in order to find the secret of life. I wanted to know how I could manipulate smoke to create life like nature does with flesh and vegetable matter. Of course, my inability to move severely hindered my attempts to explore the world. Yet, my roots run far and deep and I am able to see the world through them." Mandelbrot gestured at the roots that burrowed into his bark. "I can even see into my own body," he said with a grin. "For many years, I learned very little. Only after I had observed the land for over millions of years did I uncover a basic truth about nature. I saw that the land is much like the ocean. The soil moves like currents and the mountains swell and crash like waves."

Hectic looked hard at the mountains surrounding the valley and said, "I do not see the mountains move."

Mandelbrot laughed and said, "The brief life span of most creatures is far too short to notice the changing of mountains. One can only see the motion of mountains over millions of years."

Mandelbrot blew out a plume of smoke, which unlike the other times did not engulf Hectic. He carefully molded the smoke into a sphere, which spun slowly like a lump of clay on a wheel.

He said, "This sphere is a rough model of the world in which we live. Like smoke, the stuff of our world moves at varied rates. When we view the history of our world over the course of billions of year, we see that what seems constant is really in flux. Behold the surface of your world over billions of years." Mandelbrot swept two of his branches across the air and the speed that the sphere was spinning increased. Upon the sphere Hectic saw that what had appeared solid had taken a fluid like appearance. "This is a perspective of your world where a millions years passes in what to you feels like a second," said Mandelbrot. "What looks to you like ocean waves rising and falling is really the land pushing up into mountains and crumbling. You see, the land has currents just as the ocean does. The only difference is the waves of land exist on a larger scale of time than ocean waves.

"Now, behold the world from a perspective where one's entire life unfolds in a single second." Mandelbrot blew on his pipe and smoke came out of the bowl and infused with the sphere. The sphere's rotation slowed exponentially, and the fluid-like motion that resembled ocean waves froze into solid land. "Behold," said

Mandelbrot, "what the waves of a turbulent ocean appear as over a smaller scale of time."

Mandelbrot inhaled on his pipe. The sphere dissolved back into wisps of smoke, which streamed into the bowl of Mandelbrot's pipe and vanished. Mandelbrot became silent. He was furrowing his brow and appeared to be thinking very hard. After a long pause, he began to speak again.

"When I apprehended the complexity of nature, I decided to invent a system with which I could organize the phenomena of nature. At the time, I assumed that there was a basic building block of matter, which I decided to call the atom. I assumed that if I knew all the properties of the atom, then I could adduce all the properties of matter in general. After about a million years of observing and letting my roots grow, I found what I believed was the atom. In about a thousand years, I had systematically catalogued all the behaviors of atoms. At that point, I believed that I had complete understanding of the atom. Yet, when I went to deduce how the physical world worked from my knowledge of the atom, my conclusions did not match reality. I figured that I had missed some small detail of the atom that I could find within a matter of days. Alas, not until another thousand years of observation did I discover that the detail I had missed was that the atom was not the smallest particle."

"I found the atom was comprised of two smaller particles, which I called electrons and protons. Not until another thousand years had passed was I able to organize all the behaviors of the protons and electrons. I used my new knowledge of the subatomic particles to deduce how the physical world operates. Unfortunately, my deductions about how the physical world should work did not square with how the physical world does work. I decided to take another look at the protons and electrons to see if I had missed some small detail. Once again, I found that there were still smaller particles in what I had thought were the basic building blocks of matter."

"For the next million years, I kept searching for the smallest particle only to keep finding smaller particles. One day, I noticed there was some gray in my leafy beard. I suddenly realized that I had grown old and that I could die before I ever found the smallest particle. For the very first time, I apprehended that matter did not necessarily have to have limits. There was nothing logically impossible about the universe being infinitely large or the constituents of matter being infinitely small. I had become hyper-focused on finding the building blocks of matter and had forgotten about my original goal of creating life. I decided at that point to focus solely on the basic patterns of matter to create life."

ROOT 3.4 — HOW MANDELBROT BECAME SICK

"Over the next forty years, I intently watched how the crude induced my metabolism to evolve. I studied my physiology with keen interest to see how I would evolve under such circumstances. Overall my metabolism was geared towards getting the most energy from the crude as possible."

"Does this mean," interjected Hectic, "that you move all the materials that utilize the crude to the desert regions where the largest deposits are?"

"On the contrary," responded Mandelbrot. "My roots move the crude to where the materials are. Moving the bulky components of my metabolism that utilize the crude is energy inefficient in comparison to moving the crude. You see the crude is a liquid and is easy for my roots to transport. Moreover, even a little crude has a lot of energy. If I were to move the relatively heavy and awkward materials toward the crude instead of doing the reverse, I would lose energy. I evolved to pump the crude to the environments where I only grew before my roots found the crude. The crude flowed to where there was rich soil, clean water, abundant minerals, and mild weather. In the hospitable lands, the crude stimulated the combustion machines to process the minerals and pump the water to my higher branches.

"In the desert, I evolved special offshoots that were able to pump the maximum crude out with the minimum return of materials. The special offshoots I named despot shrubs. When these shrubs first began to grow, they sprouted silver leaves, which I called entrepreneur leaves. Next, a proliferation of bronze leaves grew, which I called labor leaves. The labor leaves proliferated wildly until they needed many more materials than my metabolism could provide for them. During this stage of the despot evolution, many of the labor leaves would die while the survivors turned brown. The new plain brown leaves I call pauper leaves. The pauper leaves were highly adept at surviving with the least amount of material. They were able to eke out an existence on the most meager supply of water and nutrients. Yet, even the hardy pauper leaves would soon proliferate beyond their food source. When a despot bush grows, the tyrannical leaf is the last leaf to grow. The immature despot bush initially contains only pauper leaves. The pauper leaves have physiologies geared towards vigorously pursuing the scarce nutrients they need to survive in the harsh desert environment. Often times there are not enough nutrients for all the leaves. During those times, the leaves produce toxins that tend to kill other leaves around them. I refer to this cycle as the internecine strife cycle. During the strife cycle, most of the despot bush sharply curtails crude production as the leaves devote most of their energy to killing each other. A crude shortage ensues, which harms my physiology as a whole. As the strife cycle continues, a tyrannical leaf forms. In the early stages, the tyrannical leaf looks identical to the pauper leaves. The only difference between the two leaves is that the tyrannical leaf produces far more toxins than the pauper leaves. In this stage of the cycle, my physiology sends enzymes into the desert region that enhances the tyrannical leaf's toxic producing ability. Soon every pauper leaf above the tyrannical leaf dies and falls off the despot shrub leaving the tyrannical leaf on top.

  The tyrannical leaf's primary function is to maintain the maximum crude flow out of the desert while keeping the flow of materials in at a minimum. The tyrant absorbs any extra energy that the bush cannot use for pumping crude. Next, the tyrant directs the energy through the roots and into far-away offshoots. The humanoid cells in the far away offshoots then harmlessly dissipate the energy through the laborious search for sparkling gems and other rare things. My metabolism then pumps the relatively small amount of rare things back to the tyrannical leaves. The high concentration of precious stones is what gives the tyrant leaf such a colorful shiny appearance.

Occasionally, a tyrannical leaf becomes overly toxic and sends toxins into some of the neighboring desert offshoots. When the neighboring peasant leaves die, the amount of crude I can produce as a whole diminishes.

My physiology has evolved a response to the overly toxic tyrannical leave, which I call a military cycle. First specialized humanoids, which I call politicians, release a catalyst called propaganda. The propaganda stimulates the more crude dependent cells to organize into large collectives called armies. At the same time, my physiology begins to produce massive amounts of specialized enzymes called weapons. The armies bind to the weapons and drift through the roots towards the desert offshoots. When the armies reach the bush, they destroy the tyrannical leaf."

Mandelbrot paused for a moment and gave Hectic a strange look. "Lately," he said, "my physiology has been producing an inordinate amount of the propaganda catalyst. I believe the propaganda infusion is the result of a worldwide dwindling of the crude supply. Just recently, my physiology initiated the military cycle against a despot bush with a tyrannical leaf that was not overly toxic. Lately I have begun to feel sick, and I don't see any way that my physiology can evolve to make me feel better."

Mandelbrot stopped speaking and stared ravenously at Hectic. As the awkward pause grew longer, Hectic began to feel uncomfortable.

"Mandelbrot, what are you going to do about your illness?" he finally asked.

"I'm going to take my medicine," snarled Mandelbrot. Mandelbrot's mouth jerked open and he shot his tongue towards Hectic like a frog eating a fly. In a split second, Mandelbrot swallowed Hectic whole.

OFFSHOOT FOUR

THE BOWELS

ROOT 4.1 — BELT 87, RP CARDS, KL2 NUMBERS, AND THE H5F MACHINE

Whack! Hectic felt his body fall flat on a hard surface. Innumerable sensations, like wisps of smoke mixed inseparably together into such an incomprehensible jumble, that his ability to filter the world crashed into a useless heap. Feelings, thoughts, impressions, sights, and sounds melted together into liquid and drowned his sensibility. The first impression that rose out of the mental mush was that he was underwater. He could only hear muffled sounds and see ambiguous shifting images around him.

As his sentience began to improve, he perceived that he was in a vast chamber. He soon realized that the chamber he was in opened into other chambers like the buds of a cauliflower head. An intangible malaise filled the air. Huge open spaces flowed into tunnels and smaller spaces as if forming a stream of consciousness that was unending, nauseating, and terrifying to behold. Paths as twisted as writhing eels shot off the ground, twisting and turning as if in pain before escaping into large tunnels high up in the walls. Smaller paths supported by thick silvery threads appeared as long parasitic worms— twisting around, wavering, threading themselves through the larger paths — before either burrowing themselves into the walls, or stretching into vast open areas.

Hectic trembled and opened his mouth slightly. He chirped weakly like a helpless baby bird that has fallen out of a nest. His auditory perception began to slowly re-assimilate, and he became vaguely aware of a dizzying hustle and bustle. As the sounds became more distinct, he recognized the clackty clack of hoofs and the clickty click of claws.

Suddenly, he was able to clearly perceive his surroundings. He saw crowds of animals wearing peculiar stiff white shirts and queer shiny black pants shuffling in every direction with lifeless eyes. Around their necks hung an odd piece of cloth that went halfway down their torso before ending in a triangle. Hectic shook his head and with quivering eyes turned fearfully about in small circles as if sharks were swimming around him.

Giant ants were crawling up the walls, down the thick silvery threads and across the walkways. They negotiated everything as easily upside-down as they did right side up. Some of the ants carried enormous stacks of rectangular leafy-like material in their mandibles. He strained his neck as he watched two ants above his heads cross paths. As they negotiated the walkway upside down, their black strips drifted into the air like limp pieces of seaweed. They silently moved their heads from side to side and ran their antennas up and down each other's bodies. Then one of them handed a stack of leafy things to the other. Hordes upon hordes of ants crawled everywhere and repeated the same strange scene— touching with feelers, heads moving from side to side, exchanging.

Objects seemed to be drifting down some of the walkways. Hectic thought that perhaps in his confused state he was experiencing delusions. He squinted and focused his eyes. This was no delusion. The walkways were actually moving and pumping brown square objects of all different sizes throughout the labyrinth. The insane walkways threaded their way through the other paths, rising and falling madly, veering erratically in every direction. Hectic seemed to float to the moving walkways as if they emanated currents that pulled him off his hooves. Hardly aware of what he was doing, he took one of the objects off the walkway. On the side of the package was the inscription Quadrant 5- Section PQ- code 103072. He flung the package back onto the belt.

What did this all mean? Hectic wondered. *Have I been unconscious for a while and how did I come to this place anyway?* He vaguely remembered Mandelbrot's gaping mouth. *Had Mandelbrot swallowed him? Was he now inside Mandelbrot's stomach? Why could he see no hole in the wall, no portal that he could have come from?* He had somehow gone from the glen with Mandelbrot to within this labyrinth.

Bweahhh! Bweahhh! A jarring sound burst out of the ocean of confusion and assaulted his ears. The moving walkways shook, and lurched forward as though they were vomiting. "Jam, jam in Belt 87," a distorted voice echoed repeatedly in mind numbing waves. Way up high, bounding from one walkway to the next, some kind of animal, a black zigzag, was bouncing frantically about. The animal looked like an ape or a monkey. *Where did the monkey-ape come from?* Hectic wondered. *Did he just materialize on the middle of the moving walkway?* The monkey-ape was frantically trying to un-jam the walkways by pushing the brown objects forward with his feet. Despite his best efforts, the objects were spilling over the side of the walkways and onto the ground below. Soon other monkey-apes were up high. They pointed with their fingers, pushed with their feet, and yelled at each another as they jumped from walkway to walkway with the utmost sense of urgency. Hectic noticed that there were now walruses shuffling about on the labyrinth floor. One walrus was standing next to where a moving walkway dipped down to ground level. Occasionally, he would take one of the objects off the belt with his flippers, and examine the inscription on the side.

Bweahhh! Bweahhh! "Jam in Belt 87," the voice repeated. The noise and confusion mushed together and pushed into Hectic's head in a thick and sickening globe. Hectic strained to pull himself together and to make sense of what was going on around him. Unfortunately, his ability to focus seemed to have vanished in all the confusion. Finally, the hideous noise stopped, the monkey-apes vanished, and the walkways resumed pumping the brown objects.

Just as Hectic was trying to regain his senses, a ringing just barely loud enough for him to hear skittled above the disarray like little water bugs. The ringing seemed to beckon Hectic. He covered one ear and tried to find what direction the noise was coming from. After some considerable effort, he discovered the source of the ringing was a strange rectangular-shaped object attached to the labyrinth wall. In the middle of the object were twelve square buttons—ten of which had numbers on them, and the two on the bottom corners had odd symbols. Jutting out from the object was a double-hooked prong, upon which hung a long handle-shaped thing with two circular knobs on either end. Coming out of the bottom knob was a strange smooth strand that coiled like an umbilical cord before re-attaching to the belly of the strange box. The ringing gave Hectic a strong impression he was supposed to do something. He began pushing the buttons but nothing happened. Then he lifted the strange handle of the box. To his amazement, an angry chittering sound spewed out of the upper knob. When he put the knob to his ear, he was flabbergasted to find that the chittering was a voice! "Hello?" he said.

"Help! I've been on the phone for hours. Phew! What a relief to get a real somebody. All I get are those damned machines, push one for this, push two for that, push this push that." The voice seemed desperate as if belonging to someone in mortal danger. On and on the chittering voice went about how he had called one number, and then was told to call another number, and then another before ending up on hold. Hectic had no idea what the voice was talking about. He would have helped the voice if he could, but what could he do? He was just a lost creature who picked up a random thing on a random wall somewhere in the labyrinth. Hectic's stomach quivered with nervousness as he anticipated telling the voice that he could not help. He would be the one that would make the voice even more miserable. The voice went on unremittingly about weird things and did not give Hectic a chance to interject.

"You see I'm having some sort of problem with my RP Card. Every time I swipe the card through the H5F Machine, a message comes on the screen that says, 'please enter your KL2 Number.' I never had to enter any K12 Number before, and I don't even have any idea what that is. I called the number on the back of the card and spoke to someone at the head of the Department of Special Problems. He said he didn't know what to do, and that I never should have been able to receive credit from an H5F Machine without my KL2 Number in the first place. He told me to call a different number, and I've been on the phone ever since." The voice paused and a dreadful silence followed that was like the moment before an execution.

"I'm sorry, I can't help you. I'm new here," Hectic said.

"No, no, no!" the voice screamed. "Don't hang up! Don't hang up!" As Hectic took the knob from his ear and put the double handle back on the hook, he wondered what "hanging up" meant. He could hear the voice screaming, "Please! Please help me!" and then as the hook sank down the voice spoke no more. Had he done something terrible? *For Pete's sake,* I must be logical about things. *Certainly I didn't kill that voice*," he thought. This place was insane and Hectic wanted out. He could feel his mind disintegrating into chaos as the confusion smothered him from all sides. He knew he had to fight the chaos if he wanted to find his way out. He could not let his irrational side get the better of him.

He would have to be logical, rational, impose order surely and strongly on the confusion around him.

ROOT 4.2 — HECTIC GETS THE RUNAROUND

That voice's problems are not my fault, Hectic thought. *There's nothing I could have done. Feeling bad won't help the voice now.* Although this was all true, these bits of logic did not seem to stop his growing anxiety from chewing away at his insides like a swarm of shrews.

He decided the first logical step was to stop one of the animals and ask for directions to an ordered place. "Sir, Sir excuse—" He tried to stop a pig in a nifty suit who was walking by him. "Excuse me sir, I was wondering if—" Before he could finish the sentence, the pig veered to the side and was quickly melded into the restless mass of bodies. Hectic did not take the pigs behavior personally. The labyrinth was extremely noisy and the pig obviously hadn't heard him. Yet, when he tried to stop some of the other animals, no matter how loudly he spoke, or how politely he approached them, he got similar responses.

Hectic grew frustrated and began to speculate why the animals were not responding to him. *Was I somehow behaving rudely? Did they all have somewhere extremely important to go?* The animals seemed to be deliberately ignoring him, and he could not understand why. He was quite certain that he had done nothing rude and could not believe that they all had somewhere very urgent to go. Their reaction was unwarranted, but even worse the animals were absurd. He could not ascribe a reason to their behavior— not even a selfish one. The pure irrationality of the animals annoyed him far more than the inconvenience they were causing him.

Hectic took a deep breath. He knew that he was just going to have to endure their absurdity. There was no other reasonable choice. He could not find his way from such a Byzantine maze without any one to help him. He was going to have to get directions from someone.

"Pardon me," he said to a passing female zebra. Like the others, she passed right by him. Determined, Hectic hastened after her before she escaped into the confusion. "Excuse me, excuse me," he repeatedly said, as he walked right next to her. She continued to look lifelessly ahead. He ran in front of her and blocked her path. "Excuse me!" he yelled. The zebra stopped dead and looked trembling upward at Hectic as if he had just slapped her out of a deep sleep. "Oh, I'm terribly sorry," blurted Hectic. "I didn't mean to startle you. I just…I have…please, please, help me. I'm completely confused. I don't think I'm where I intended. I'm not sure how I got in here. This place is so strange. I've got to get out." She said nothing for a moment, gazing at Hectic dumbfounded. Then her mouth formed a little black hole, and the words spilled from her in dizzying rapidness.

"Oh, oh, oh, your new here aren't you?"

"Yes I am. Do you—"

"Where are you trying to go?" she interrupted.

Hectic thought for a moment. "I want to go to place with order," he finally said. "I must get to an ordered place or I will go crazy. Do you know the way?"

"Yes," said the zebra after a thoughtful pause. "The Ordered Place is on the top floor, although, I couldn't tell you how to get there, for I don't know the way. If you want directions there, you need to register."

"Register, what does that mean?" asked Hectic.

"You need to go to the Administration Office to get registered. Unfortunately, I haven't been there for a while and I have forgotten where the office is. However, there's an information booth in Sector 42m. They should certainly be able to tell you where the Administration Office is."

"42m?"

"Oh silly me, how would you know where that is either? What you do is you go to that tunnel over there that slopes steeply upward. Take your second right, follow that corridor until you see the IU8 stair case, take that to the YP overpass, make a left at the...." and on and on she went. Hectic strained to understand what she was saying. Unfortunately, the strain of trying to focus in the labyrinth of distraction had sapped his energy. Her words melted together into a senseless puddle within his head. As she continued to talk, a buzzing noise burst into the air and startled him. He whipped around to see what the noise was and saw nothing. When he had turned back around, the zebra was gone. He glanced about, trying frantically to find her. She seemed to have simply melted into the restless masses of animals like a drop of water in an ocean. All he could do now was try to remember what she had told him.

All he could remember was the first two steps of the directions. These he said to himself repeatedly as if he were blowing on two little sparks that were about to go out within the chaos of his head. After he had followed them through to completion, he stopped several other animals and asked for directions to the information booth but learned nothing. Even if his concentration were not suffocating to death, he would not have understood any of them. Their directions were like giant balls of tangled string that no one could unravel.

Only through sheer chance did he stumble on a small closet sized booth that sprung out of the ground like a horse's tooth. Above the booth in big letters, was the word INFORMATION. He did not quite understand how this tiny building supplied information. "Was there somebody within who would tell him everything he wanted to know? Were the directions written on the inside wall?" He leaned over the counter to try and see what was inside. As he did so, an Afghanistan hound shot upward from the floor like a bursting bubble. He glared at Hectic as though he had interrupted him in the middle of doing something very personal.

"Can I help you sir?" he snapped. Hectic staggered backwards, opening and closing his mouth like a dying fish. "Sir, is there something I can help you with?"

"Yes," Hectic responded, as he gestured weakly with his human arm. "I'm looking for the Administration Office."

"The Administration Office? Humph, and which one might that be? There are hundreds you know."

"Uhhh, I don't know which one. I'm completely lost. I guess I need the one for those who have never registered before." The hound looked away and began fiddling with his paws, as though he had forgotten all about Hectic. As the moments passed by, Hectic began to shift nervously in place. He was not quite sure what he was supposed to do. Did he somehow offend the hound? No, he could think of nothing he had done that was offensive. He did not deserve this hound's rude behavior. Yet, for whatever reason the hound had decided to ignore him. Hectic began to get angry. He could not stand this pointless wasting of time. He cleared his throat and prepared to give that dog a piece of his mind. Before he could say a word however, the hound jerked forward nearly hitting him in the face.

"You don't need the Administration Office," he barked. "You need the Registration Office, probably the one in Sector RB."

"The what?"

"What you want to do is—" and then there was a long recitation of convoluted directions, uttered in such blazing speed Hectic could scarcely understand a word. When the hound finished, he shot back down into the information booth and vanished from sight.

Hectic wandered away in a state of senility. He had no mental energy left to think. He had exhausted himself in the futile effort of trying to get directions, suppressing his anxiety, and attempting to thing logically in all the confusion. Registration Office, Sector RB; Registration Office, Sector RB—these words fluttered about in his heads like little specks of ash above the flames of a raging fire. He walked about aimlessly in a dizzy haze, unable to concentrate on where he was going or what he should do next. Suddenly, he found himself teetering on the edge of a walkway high above the floor. Just a blink of an eye ago, he was at the information booth, and the unexpected surprise of finding himself so high caused him to jerk backwards and nearly catapult himself off the edge. He swung his mismatched arms wildly and regained his balance.

The throngs of animals below were far enough down that Hectic could not distinguish one from the other. They looked like a great mass of digesting food churning in a gigantic stomach. Hectic became dizzy looking at the restless mobs shifting amorphously down below. He quickly turned away and walked over the high walkway to a tunnel in the wall.

He continued down countless paths and tunnels where he stopped numerous animals for directions. At last, his efforts paid off. He was navigating a hallway so narrow that he had to turn sideways just to proceed through. In this position, his eyes just happened to fall on a leafy thing stuck to the wall. R̲E̲G̲I̲S̲T̲R̲A̲T̲I̲O̲N̲ O̲F̲F̲I̲C̲E̲,̲ S̲E̲C̲T̲O̲R̲ R̲B̲ read the leafy thing. A little arrow below the message pointed down the hall. Hectic breathed a sigh of relief, for his nightmare would soon be over. Soon he would register, go to the top, and find the ordered land. He followed arrows around various turns and curves. Eventually, he turned a corner and entered a hallway tightly crammed with animals. *Where had they all come from?* he wondered. He had not seen any animals in the narrow corridor where he had just been. Hectic walked a few steps forward, towards the crowd. The mass of animals seemed to engulf him like an amoeba eating a tiny piece of biological matter.

Hectic stood up straight and peered over the other animal's heads. He noticed that at the beginning of the heap, there was an opening in the wall. In the opening sat a giant ant who was busy plucking away at various buttons and staring at a big glowing box. Hectic concluded that this was the line to the Registration Office and that he would simply have to wait his turn to register.

rootlet 4.21 — the registration office

More animals shuffled in behind Hectic and crowded him with their bodies. The line slowly moved him forward in rhythmic motions like a snake swallowing prey. The air became extremely stuffy and unpleasant. Hectic could smell animal musk, the mustiness of starchy clothes, and a sickening sweet smell that seemed to emanate from the animals' hair and limb pits. He was starting to feel anxious and claustrophobic. He wanted desperately to leave the stuffy hall and go somewhere quiet to catch his breath. However, Hectic was slowly drawing closer to the front of the line. He knew that leaving the hall would be irrational. He would only have to return later and start his wait all over again. All he had to do was wait a bit longer. The problem was that he did not know how much longer and part of him felt that he might be in line forever. The line seemed to have stopped moving. Hectic began to burn with frustration as if wrapped in a blanket saturated with boiling water. His legs were starting to ache and he was feeling lightheaded.

      He repeatedly reminded himself to be rational and to stay in line. Eventually, the line did resume a slow crawl forward. Soon thereafter, Hectic noticed that there were only five animals left in front of him. He had managed to successfully wait in line and now he was close to registering. The first three animals went quickly. Only an ostrich and a rhino remained in front of him. Unfortunately, the dreadful bird was taking an inordinate amount of time. Whatever he wanted must have been extremely complicated. The administrator kept leaving the window and returning with different papers, which he would lay in front of the ostrich. The insect would then point out various sections on the papers with a small blue stick. The ostrich always responded by leaning forward and scrutinizing whatever the ant was showing him. Every few seconds the ostrich would nod significantly as if he had understood something very important. Always though he would ask something else, which would again prompt the ant to go to the back and get more papers. Then the entire ridiculous process would start over again.

     Hectic again became angry. "How much longer can this take?" he wondered. He felt as if he was drowning in frustration. The waiting, the unbearable smells, the cramped hallway were driving him insane. His mind became unfocused and began to whir with questions and thoughts. "Why wasn't the office located in one of the large open spaces? Why didn't they have more insects on duty?" He tried to calm himself down but could not. Instead, he grew more and more agitated. An overwhelming urge to smack the ostrich on his stupid, bald, head began to consume him. He imagined how satisfying the smack would feel on his bear claw, how delightful to see that small ugly head bounce off the window ledge. He gleefully envisioned blood pouring out of the ostrich's mangled beak. He looked at the ground and tried not to think of the ordered paradise that was just out of his reach.

When he had finally managed to think of something else, his mental wanderings were interrupted by the ant who was saying, "Sir, sir, sir!"

"Hmmm," said Hectic.

"Can I help you?"

"Oh I'm sorry. I didn't realize my turn had come. I would like to register to go to the top."

"You mean this is your first time?"

"Yes, I was wonder—"

"Well, then you are going to have to fill out a blue form. Hold on one moment please."

The ant got off his chair and slowly crawled towards the back room. *How strange,* Hectic thought. *Why should registering for the first time be unusual? Everyone who registers must have had a first time at some point. Why doesn't he have the blue forms somewhere close by?*

From behind him came the sounds of disgruntled snorts and hardly audible growls. The animals were getting annoyed at the amount of time he was taking. Hectic began to shift nervously in place while he stared into the office to try to see what the insect was doing. The place was swarming with ants. They meticulously took stacks of papers in their mandibles and handed them to one another. They crept and crawled out of back entrances and interacted without emotion. Sometimes they put their black glassy eyes inches from each other, slowly opened and closed their mandibles, moved their heads from side to side, and felt each other with their antennas.

"Oh, you need a writing implement. Hold on just a moment." The insect ducked from sight behind the counter, and popped back up holding a small smooth blue stick with a silvery point at one end. He released the blue stick from his mandibles and let the thing drop on the counter top. As Hectic picked up the stick with his human hand, he puzzled over what the insect wanted him to do. "Sir, please hurry and fill out the information on the forms," urged the insect. "You're holding up the whole line."

Hectic looked at the leafy things. On them were certain questions. *Ah ha*! thought Hectic. So this was what he was supposed to do. He took the little blue writing implement and began to scribble the answers next to the questions. With some of the sections, he had no problem. Some of the others sections, however, were more confusing. One section asked for his Kl2 Number and his Place of Entry. "What did all this mean?" Hectic asked for the assistance of the giant ant. The ant responded by pointing out various sections and subsections—which clarified absolutely nothing—with his spindly appendage. Hectic did not want to appear to be holding up the line because he was stupid. He stood there nodding his hybrid head as if everything the ant was indicating was perfectly clear. Hectic would then rephrase the same questions over and over to at least sound like he was saying something new. The insect was now pushing the numerous buttons in front of him. Each of the buttons was labeled with a letter, and when the insect pushed one, the letter would appear on the surface of the box.

    The animals behind him were becoming increasingly more restless. Hectic could hear them growling louder and louder. He was holding up the whole line. If only the insect would hurry. The ant eventually stopped pushing buttons on his computer and put both his spindly appendages behind his head.

"I can't help you," he said. "Your K12 Number is restricted. I will have to send you to see Mr. Tantalus. He's head of the Special Problems Division. Just go through the second door on your right."

"But all I want to do is—"

"Next." A raccoon cut in front of Hectic and handed the insect a stack of leafy things. Hectic sighed and walked away from the administrator completely dismayed. All he could do now was find Mr. Tantalus's office and hope there were no lines. He took the second right like the administrator had told him to and ended up in a hall, which split like a Y. To the left was a narrow flight of stairs that went up, and to the right was a narrow flight of stairs that went down. Hectic hesitated. The ant had not mentioned anything about a split in the hall, and Hectic wasn't sure which direction to go. He decided to take the stairs that went down. A few twists and turns later Hectic was completely lost again. He sat down in a narrow hall with his back against the wall and began to cry.

After a little while, an ant rounded the corner and headed towards the sobbing Hectic. The ant walked right over him, oblivious to the fact that there was somebody sitting in the middle of the hall having a break down. The feel of the spindly little legs touching him jolted Hectic out of his sorrowful stupor. He stopped crying, and when another ant rounded the corner Hectic yelled out to him. "Excuse me, could you tell me where Mr. Tantalus' office is?" The insect continued towards Hectic without saying anything. When he reached Hectic, he stopped and began feeling the entire length of Hectic's body with his antennas.

"Can I help you?" he finally said.

"Yes," said Hectic testily. "Can you tell me where Mr. Tantalus' office is?"

The bug paused for a minute and circled his antennas in the air. "Your second right down, then your first left," he uttered. He then walked nonchalantly over Hectic just as the first insect had.

No matter, Hectic thought. *I'll get to this insect's office and get out of this crazy place.*

rootlet 4.22 — Mr. Tantalus

Hectic got up and proceeded to follow the insect's directions. He took the second right and then the first left. The hallway narrowed until Hectic could hardly progress forward. As he continued, the hallway became rounded. The walls took on a strange grayish-pink color and were wrinkled with numerous cracks and fissures. Hectic felt as if he was a piece of food passing through an intestinal tract. Farther down the hall, a giant metal pipe emerged from the ceiling and ran along the top of the hall. Hectic had to duck down under the pipe and continue on his hands and knees. Every once in a while, the pipe emitted a muffled, rumbling sound that caused the entire hallway to vibrate.

After he had crawled a substantial distance, Hectic heard the familiar plickety-plick of someone pressing letter buttons. Up ahead a sallow light emanated from an entranceway on the side of the tunnel. As Hectic approached, he saw a sign next to the entranceway that read: MR. TANTALUS, HEAD OF THE DEPARTMENT OF SPECIAL PROBLEMS. Hectic entered the office and stood up.

A large rickety desk nearly filled the entire office and hardly left any room for Hectic to stand. Behind the desk sat another ant, one long and skinny even by insect standards. The ant was slumped down in a chair as if his body was nothing more than a pile of half-melted snow. He was focusing on a huge stack of papers that he held only inches from his mandibles. His shirt looked ready to slide off his narrow shoulders, and was bunched up around his lower thorax like a bulldog's face. He either did not notice or did not care to respond to Hectic, who stood in front of him for quite awhile. Eventually, his antennas began rotating slowly on his head. Without looking up, he said, "Can I help you?"

"Yes, there seems to be some problem with my registration, I'm not sure what I—"

"Name," the insect interrupted.

"Hectic," said Hectic. The insect plicked the little letter buttons that spelled the name upon the surface of the glowing box. He gazed at the screen for a very long time in a kind of dreary drained way.

"Mmmm," he said, nodding his head in a reaffirming manner.

"Do you see the problem?" asked Hectic.

"Yes I do," the bug replied. Hectic stood silently, twitching, waiting for the spindly little insect to give him an answer. Finally, he grew impatient and asked timidly,

"What's the problem?"

The insect turned and gave him a sour look, as if he had asked something very rude. Then, he took the glowing box in his spindly appendages and rotated the screen slowly towards Hectic. The box creaked as if resisting rotation and the insect groaned as if making a great effort. When the screen was facing Hectic, he let out a giant weary sigh. The ant's bony little chest sank impossibly far inward, and for a second the ant looked like he might implode.

"See here," he said abruptly thrusting his tiny little appendage into the screen. Where he pointed was written:

<u>HECTIC, OUT OF ORDER</u>.

"Out of Order," said Hectic. "What does that mean?"

"What does that mean?" echoed the ant. "Well, either you are dead, or you never existed in the first place. This happens all the time."

The ant's explanation momentarily stultified Hectic, who stood silently staring into space. Then he began to chuckle uneasily. "I am clearly alive," he said, "and I am standing right in front of you."

The insect shook his head impatiently. "No! You grossly oversimplify the situation," snapped the insect. "The very fact that you're up and walking about does not mean anything. We need some proof that you exist. Somebody needs to register you on this computer. Or at the very least, I need some official documents to grant me the authority to register you."

"Why can't you just type my name in?" Hectic asked.

"Why can't you just type my name in," mimicked the insect in the wildly oscillating cadence of sarcasm. The ant shrugged his knobby little shoulders and extended his appendages outward in an exaggerated fashion. "As I said before, the difficulty you are having is quite common and therefore does not fall under the purview of this department. I simply am not equipped to handle common problems. Common problems tend to be more difficult to solve, which is why they tend to be around with such frequency. What you need is a department that specializes in your particular common problem. I suggest you make an appointment with the Department of Misapplied Names and Labels in Sector QZ."

The ant abruptly stopped talking and went back to plicking away at his keyboard. Hectic felt confused and stood waiting for Mr. Tantalus to give him further instruction. After a short spell of silence the insect said, "I think we're finished here." The bug seemed impatient to resume his important job of plucking the letter buttons, and staring at the dull screen.

"Can you at least tell me where the office is located?" asked Hectic sharply.

Mr. Tantalus shifted his seat a little bit to the left, revealing a small hole in the wall behind him. "You just go through this little hallway," he said. "This will take you right back to the Registration Office from where you came. They will tell you how to get to the DMNL. I don't know why you didn't come here that way in the first place. You would have gotten here much more quickly."

Hectic was skeptical if the tunnel really did lead back to the registrar. In all likelihood, there were many registrars within the giant labyrinth. "How could Mr. Tantalus know from which registrar he had come?" He wanted to ask, but then he saw that the insect had gone back to work on his glowing box. He certainly didn't want to endure any more of the insect's abuse. Furthermore, there was no way he was going to remember all the twists and turns he had taken to get here. The tunnel at least provided a possibility that he would get back to the Registration Office. Hectic proceeded to crawl carefully over the top of the desk. He did not want to knock over any of the leafy stacks that the irascible ant had piled there. The bug made no effort to get out of the way. He wouldn't even shift his upper body a little bit to the side. Instead, he sat firmly in place plucking away at the buttons. Hectic twisted and turned around him before falling face-first on to the floor. As he maneuvered into position where he could enter the hole, his human arm scraped against Mr. Tantalus's body. Hectic cringed as he felt the hard little knobs and scratchy hairs scrape his body through the ant's starchy white shirt. Hectic slipped into the tunnel and began to crawl forward. He was confused as to why the labyrinth would design such an absurdly tiny tunnel. Perhaps the tiny passageway was an escape route. However, Mr. Tantalus had indicated that the passageway was a common throughway. *Why would the labyrinth develop a major throughway which one had to crawl through on all fours?* he wondered. The more he thought about the intent of the tunnel's designers the more aggravated he became. He continued forward grumbling as he went. Behind him, the sound of Mr. Tantalus' typing grew more distant.

    The tunnel was perfectly round and gently rolled in various directions like a wormhole. As Hectic progressed, the faint light from Mr. Tantalus' office gradually dimmed until he was in complete darkness. Hectic groped his way forward into the silent darkness. The tunnel seemed to be getting even smaller. Eventually, the slowly shrinking tunnel forced Hectic to get on his stomach and progress forward by wiggling like a worm. Suddenly, Hectic felt the walls tighten violently around him like a constricting throat. He could neither move forward nor backwards. "Help me!" he shrieked. He tried to scream again but the tunnel had further constricted and had squeezed all the air out of him. As he struggled for breath, he realized that he was going to die in the process of registering.

rootlet 4.23 — Hectic receives a kl2 card

Hectic did not die. Although, how he escaped was a mystery. He remembered the walls crushing him, and then suddenly he had arrived at the end of the tunnel. When he regained his senses, Hectic was in a room that looked identical to the Registration Office he was at before. The only difference was there were even more ants, hordes of them in shiny black pants and stiff white shirts, carrying huge stacks of papers in their mandibles. They crawled over their desks and each other. They scurried across the ceilings in a network of lines to and from a myriad of tunnels that honeycombed the entire room. They made no noise except for the disconcerting, rapid pittering of their spindly legs on the hard surface.

Hectic tried to get their attention, but they seemed to ignore him. He remembered that politeness had gotten him nowhere since he had entered the labyrinth. Instead of suffering the previous indignities, he grabbed one of the bugs with his powerful bear arm. "Tell me!" he demanded. "Is this the Registration Office?"

From the captured insect he discovered that he had arrived at the wrong Registration Office. Conveniently enough, however, the Department of Misapplied Names and Labels was just down the hall. Unfortunately, Hectic discovered they were unable to help him. They told him that his problem was special and fell under the jurisdiction of the Department of Special Problems. When the ant speaking to Hectic mentioned Mr. Tantalus, Hectic interrupted him. He informed the ant that he had just been to the DSP and Mr. Tantalus had told him to come here. The insect frowned, sighed wearily, picked up a ringing thing, and pushed some numbered buttons. He talked into the ringing thing for a very long time. When he was finished, he informed Hectic that neither the DSP, nor the DMNL could handle his problem. Fortunately, however, the DXSP (Department of Extra Special Problems) was just around the corner. "Certainly they will be able to help you with your problem," assured the ant.

Hectic headed around the corner with great skepticism, but he was pleasantly surprised to find that the DXSP was indeed around the corner just as the ant had said. Even better the insect on duty was actually helpful.

"Oh yes." he said cordially. "You are at the right place, and I would be delighted to help you." The insect picked up a stack of light blue papers and handed them to Hectic. "Please read and initial each page," he instructed Hectic.

Hectic skimmed through the pages and initialed where he believed he was supposed to. When he was finished, he handed the stack back to the ant. The ant stood up on his two hind legs and held the stack with his middle legs. He licked the end of his top right leg, which he then used to leaf through the pages. When he finished reading one page, he used his top left leg to put the paper at the back of the stack and continued reading the next page. The ant found several places that Hectic had overlooked and had not initialed. The ant made an X on these spots and handed the pages back to Hectic for him to initial. Eventually the ant had perused through the entire stack and was satisfied that Hectic had properly initialed each page. He put the stack in his mandibles and scurried up the wall and into a hole.

A moment later, he came back out of the hole with a bigger stack of orange papers. He handed the stack to Hectic and said, "Please read and initial each page." Just as before Hectic initialed and the insect carefully checked each page. The ant again took the stack and scurried back into the hole he had went in before. A moment later, he came back out of the hole with a stack of red papers. When the entire process was finished to the ant's satisfaction, Hectic had performed the stack-initialing protocol seven different times with seven stacks of different colored papers. At that point, he was utterly aggravated because many of the sections he had read and initialed were presented several times in each stack. His human hand ached from writing and his eyes hurt from reading all the small print. He bated his anger however, because he did not want to upset the ant and jeopardize his passage to the top. After all, he had triumphed over the process of registering. Hectic stood there looking expectantly at the ant.

"Well," said Hectic, "I'm ready to ascend to the top of the labyrinth."

"You will receive the directions out of The Bowels to the Ordered Land by mail in 6 to 10 days from now," stated the insect brusquely.

Hectic froze and began to shake. The fur on his face and bear arm bristled. "By mail! Six to ten days from now! What in the forest are you talking about?" You imbecile!" he bellowed. "I'll starve to death by the time you ants are finished pushing papers around. I haven't eaten anything since Mandelbrot ate me. Why can't you just hand me the damn directions? Why do we have to screw around and go through all this crap? You ants have bounced me all over this place and now you're going to tell me that I have to wait six to ten days. You miserable insect!" he roared.

"Sir, yelling at me is irrational. I'm only doing my job."

"Irrational. You're telling me I'm irrational. Don't you see I am going to die of starvation? There are no roots or berries in this place. What the hell am I supposed to eat?"

"Well, I don't know about roots and berries, but there is a refreshment stand around the corner," replied the ant.

"A what stand?" asked Hectic

"A refreshment stand," replied the ant. "Mr. Norder, everything is just fine."

"The insect reached into a drawer and pulled out a small, rectangular, sliver card. "Here's your kl2 card," he said.

"My what?" asked Hectic.

The flustered Hectic continued to converse for quite a while with the enigmatic insect. He believed he was making good progress in discovering from the ant exactly what he had to do to get to the top. However, when the insect had finished talking and crawled away, Hectic began to feel a little uneasy. The ant had seemed clear, and yet Hectic felt confused. He slowly realized that the ant had created the illusion of clarity with the subtle use of hedge words like "maybe," "probably," or "perhaps." In the end, all Hectic had understood was that he could somehow use the Kl2 Card to get food. He decided to go to the refreshment stand and see what he could surmise. If he could at least get some food and satiate his hunger, perhaps his hybrid head would think a bit clearer.

Hectic went to the refreshment stand and helplessly handed his card to a squirrel standing behind the counter. The squirrel snatched the card from his hand and ran up a pole to a little box-like device on the ceiling. The squirrel whipped the card through a slit on the device's side. The device beeped and buzzed before producing a rectangular piece of paper. The squirrel stuffed the piece of paper in his mouth and ran back down the pole. He looked at Hectic with his swollen cheeks before reaching into his mouth with his little claw. He pulled out the piece of paper and a small black stick. He handed the stick to Hectic and told him to sign his name on a faint blue line on the paper. When Hectic finished signing, the squirrel flung the card back down on the table and snatched the leafy thing away.

"Where is my food?" asked Hectic. The squirrel chittered angrily and dove down beneath the counter. When he popped back up, he was holding a large cylinder, which was completely white save for the black-lettered words: CANNED GOODS. Mystified, Hectic took the cylinder from the squirrel. He noticed there was a handle of sorts that lay flush against the circular top of the cylinder. He wedged one of his dagger-like bear claws underneath the handle and pulled up. The top bent and partially separated from the can with a slight scraping noise. Hectic peeled the top completely of the cylinder. Inside was a moist, densely-packed, grayish-brown, substance that smelled pungent and salty. Hectic took a leap of faith and assumed the gunk was food. He began to scoop the slop out of the cylinder and into his mouth with two of his human fingers. He could not tell if the unappetizing mush was plant, meat, or something in between. As he continued to eat, his insides began to feel strange, as if his stomach's lining was coated with slime. When he had finished eating, his stomach rumbled and he broke wind very noisily. Yet, he also felt full and re-energized. With new focus, he stormed back towards the office farting noisily as he went.

rootlet 4.24 — sector 92, quadrant 71 section g197

When Hectic returned the office, the ant who he had last spoken to was gone. Undaunted, he accosted several other ants. He was very careful to analyze every word that came out of their mandibles. When he heard a word like "maybe" or "probably," he would ask more questions and force the ants to give concrete answers. Hectic did not relent until he was sure the ants had told him something meaningful. Furthermore, he made sure he learned the names of the insects he was talking with before they had a chance to scurry away. If there were any discrepancies, he wanted to be able to find the ants responsible for the confusion.

After extensive browbeating, Hectic learned there were several routes to the top. However, because of the unfathomable complexity of The Bowels he would never be able to reach the top without directions. Furthermore, for reasons that the ants never explained — although he asked several times — he could not arrive at the top through any route. The Bowels assigned one particular route to each animal depending upon where they entered, and at what time they entered. In the meanwhile, he could get food and supplies with his K12 Card.

An insect led Hectic to a small abode called an apartment in Sector 92, Quadrant 71, Section g187. He informed Hectic that a mail carrier would push the directions through a small slit in the door some time during the next ten days. Inside the apartment were all sorts of odd devices that made strange humming and beeping noises. Hectic suspected that the devices served different sorts of practical purposes. Unfortunately, he could neither deduce nor imagine what those purposes might be. After a while, he began to grab animals as they walked by his apartment and drag them inside where he could bombard them with questions.

"What is this? What does that do? What is this for?" he would ask as he pointed to the various machines. The animals looked at him as if he was completely insane, but more often than not, they gave him some answers before announcing that they had some place important to go and that they had better be on their way. Hectic was most amazed at the strange chair that made his excrement disappear. The chair had a large hole in the seat, which was directly above a big bowl of water. Hectic learned that he was supposed to sit on the chair and defecate into the bowl of water. Then, he would push a lever, and the water would form a small whirlpool that spun his filth in circles. Next, the bowl made a gurgling sound and swallowed the water with his filth away. Lastly, the bowl miraculously re-filled with water and stood ready for the next deposit. In one room with a shiny white floor, a great white box made a quiet whirring noise. The box had two doors, which opened into two separate compartments. The compartment on top was as cold as a mid winter's night, and the one below was as cool as a fall evening.

Hectic learned he could buy all the food he needed at certain Bowel Stations. He ingeniously decided to keep the food in the great white container where the cold would prevent spoilage and decomposition. For cooking, he did not need a fire. There was a curious square container with a translucent door. Hectic learned he could use the container to cook food. First, he placed food inside the container and closed the door. Next, he pressed a few numbered buttons on the containers front side. The container would respond with a whirring noise and slowly spin the food. In this mysterious fireless way the food would cook.

Hectic's existence—with his magic card and his apartment's amenities—should have been an easy one as he waited for his directions to arrive. Unfortunately, he soon experienced a novel and unpleasant emotion that spoiled his wait: boredom. The novelty of his apartment soon wore thin, and Hectic took to pacing violently back and forth within the constraining white walls. Although he knew that he could not find the top without his directions, he was increasingly more tempted to try. Eventually the temptation became too great. In what would become a regular pattern, Hectic let out a scream and dashed out the door. In these desperate excursions into the chaos of The Bowels, he always got lost. Often, he spent hours traipsing helplessly through the madness. By the time he eventually found his way back, he could not think. For the chaos that he had endured thoroughly poisoned his mind's womb. His head birthed millions of fleeting, inchoate thoughts that all screamed for him to pluck them from oblivion. All Hectic could do was collapse as he clutched his hybrid-head between his claw and hand. There on the floor, he would groan as the din of images flickered through his heads in rapid succession. When he recovered, he always vowed to not seek the top until he had the directions to guide him.

He was not exactly sure when ten days were up. For in the sunless enclosure, there was no way to know when a day ended or began. Furthermore, no matter when he left his apartment, the activity level was always the same. There was always beeping, buzzing, screeching, belts moving, and throngs of animals passing by. Hectic tried to keep track of the days by keeping count of how many times he went to bed. He decided that every time he woke up a new day had begun.

When he had finished his tenth sleeping session, he was utterly dismayed to find his directions had not arrived. Hectic had not entertained the possibility that his directions wouldn't arrive and was at a complete loss as for what he should do. He could not believe that the insects would forget something so important. Perhaps ten days really hadn't elapsed. Hectic let several more sleeping sessions pass, and still the directions did not arrive.

He stormed back to the office of Mr. Quibblestein — the ant who had originally assured him his directions would arrive in ten days. When he arrived at the office, Mr. Quibblestein was nowhere in sight. Another ant on duty — a Mr. Milquetoast — identified himself as Mr. Quibblestein's secretary.

"Where is your manager?" Hectic asked Mr. Milquetoast.

"I'm sorry," said Mr. Milquetoast meekly. "He's in a meeting right now. He won't be available till later."

Hectic returned to the office several times over the next few days only to find that Mr. Quibblestein was never there. He was, according to Mr. Milquetoast, always in a meeting. Fifteen days later, Mr. Milquetoast timidly informed Hectic that Mr. Quibblestein had transferred to a different office and could no longer assist Hectic with his directions. He referred Hectic to a Mr. Parse whose office was only a short walk away. Mr. Parse informed Hectic that what was supposed to come in the mail for him was technically a map and not directions. He referred Hectic to the DM (Department of Maps).

The ants — with their convoluted, shifting, and bureaucratic rituals — bounced Hectic from office to office. Although the latest setback infuriated Hectic, he remained undaunted. In addition to demanding the name of every insect he spoke with, he also demanded copies of all the forms the ants had him fill out. There were stacks of them, and he brought every single one back to his apartment. The papers collected in disheveled heaps upon the furniture and tables before spilling upon the floor like forest debris.

On the thirtieth day of his existence in The Bowels, Hectic was no closer to locating the elusive directions. Furthermore, he had a serious problem with his magic card when he attempted to purchase some food. The chipmunk behind the counter ran his card through the small slit, and the device made an angry buzzing noise.

"I'm sorry, you don't have enough points to cover this," said the chipmunk.

"What! What do you mean?" responded Hectic incredulously.

"I mean your card has no credit left. Your card is useless. You can't get any food here."

"I-I...was not aware that there was any limit to the amount of food I could purchase," Hectic stammered nervously. "Please, let me get some food this one time. I could do some work for you in return if you like."

"I'm afraid I can't do that."

"I imagine that this is contrary to your typical procedure, but can't you make an exception?"

"I'm sorry, I'm afraid that's just impossible."

"Don't do this to me! I'll starve to death!"

"Sir, please, please try and be rational. I'm only doing my job," the chipmunk chittered. "I'm sorry, there's nothing I can do."

The distraught Hectic left the store hungry, empty-handed, and empty-clawed. However, he did not starve. He remembered that he had enough frozen meals in the giant white box to sustain him for a good three to four days. He was still deeply worried. He suspected he would have to undergo a long convoluted process to resolve his magic card problem, and his food would run out in the meantime.

ROOT 4.3 — THE CHAMBER OF BELTS

Three days later, Hectic was sitting in his apartment with his magic card dilemma still unresolved. Suddenly his apartment door flew open, and a fox wearing a spiffy black suit and carrying a briefcase barged in. The fox bowed majestically and clicked open his briefcase. He took out some papers and handed them to Hectic with a flourish. The fox then clicked his briefcase closed and abruptly left the apartment without saying a word. The papers said the following:

LOADERS WANTED

Earn points for your magic card as you wait to get to the top.

The Chamber of Belts is now taking applications.

Follow the belts as the packages go down to reach the application center.

Hectic decided to immediately go to the application center. He left his apartment and followed the closest belt down through cascading chambers, twisted tunnels, and tangled paths — down towards the bottom of The Bowels. The belt continued to hover a few feet above the ground before curving upward and sneaking through a hole in the wall above a set of double doors. Hectic went through the doors. As they swung shut behind him, the contrasting silence of the long narrow hallway instantly swallowed him. The only thing he heard was the slight humming noise of the belt moving overhead. As he continued down the hall, he heard a lulling soft sound like an ocean weltering in the distance. As he continued towards the double doors at the other side of the hall, the weltering became louder. When he opened the double doors, a tidal wave of noise and flashing lights engulfed him. The hall flowed into a long rectangular concrete ditch that drained into a massive chamber. On either side of him, at regular intervals, were a series of hard silvery stairs that were almost as steep as ladders.

    The noise in the chamber, although louder than anywhere else in The Bowels, did not afflict him with the same sense of confusion. The noise was a uniform entity, which did not exhaust his mind like hundreds of baby sounds vying simultaneously for his attention. Visually however, chaos poked from every crevice like prairie dogs from a colony of infinite size. Every belt in The Bowels descended to this place, a slithering horde of snakes going to hibernate for the winter. Wires intermeshed through the air, as if they were thousands of tangled roots struggling for nutrients in cluttered soil. Innumerably more monkey-apes bounded about here than he had seen anywhere else. Hectic could not be certain, however, if there actually were more of them. He had trouble discerning if his eyes were following the same monkey-ape, a different one, or a mere shadow of one. Their images flashed in and out of existence through the flickering lights, and their usual frantic movements appeared more desperate than ever.

In this chamber, the snake-work of belts was perpetually clogged with an overabundance of packages. The overwhelmed monkey-apes could not keep up. As a result, they were in a constant state of frustration. Hectic became dizzy as the innumerable flickering images of their clenched-pointed teeth, hairy arms waving in the air, and frantic head-shaking besieged him.

Numerous walruses at the base of the floor bumped into each other as they shuffled ponderously about. They took those packages that had fallen to the floor and attempted to put them back on the correct belts. Most of the belts were too high up for them to reach. The walruses' response was to awkwardly hurl the packages at the monkey-apes, who were gesturing wildly for the walruses to hurry. More often than not, the walruses missed their target; and the packages rained down like giant hail. Hectic noticed that there were hundreds of phones interspersed throughout the chamber. On each one there was a walrus or a monkey-ape. They covered their extra ear with their appendage and concentrated with strained faces as they tried in vain to hear the voice on the other end. In all the sickening confusion, Hectic's eyes became tired and he lost the ability to focus. The images became blurry like wavering wisps of smoke dissipating into each other. Hectic brought his bear-claw and hand to the sides of his head and blocked his peripheral vision. He focused his view straight down the ditch and protected his mind from the groping claws of distraction as best he could.

As he steadily progressed forward, he saw the wavering image of an ant down the ditch in the darkness at the other end of the chamber. He was not quite sure if he was looking at an actual ant or merely the shadow of one. The shadowy ant waved him forward with a stringy appendage. Hectic advanced, but as he drew near the ant-shadow receded backwards into the darkness and disappeared. "What do you want?" yelled Hectic. He rushed towards the shadow where the antlike image had vanished. In the dim light, he saw another pair of doors identical to the ones through which he had entered the chamber. He went through the doors, which swung shut and swallowed him into a stomach of silence. He was in a strange dark tunnel that started out large and got increasingly smaller like a funnel. At the distant smaller end, Hectic could see the shadowy image of the insect waving him forward. When Hectic inched forward, the insect apparition faded into the blackness. As he walked farther into the funnel, he had to stoop lower: First, he bent his head; and then, his back; and then he had to crawl on all fours. Eventually he had to wiggle on his stomach in the pitch-black wormhole. At the narrow end of the tunnel, there was a sharp turn. Hectic tried to squirm through, but he could only get his human hand and hybrid-head halfway through the turn: The rest of his body was too big to follow. In his twisted position, he could see that the tunnel became dramatically bigger after the turn. On the enlarging wall shinned a bright light in the shape of a right triangle. Hectic could hear the plickity-plick-plick of someone typing and the rustling of papers.

"Hello!" Hectic shouted. "Does somebody want to talk to me?" The plicking stopped, but no one responded to him. He was about to shout louder when suddenly the elongated shadow of an ant emerged on the triangle.

"You have come looking for work to earn points?" asked the shadow.

"Yes, I am out of points I must—"

"You must fill out some papers first," interrupted the shadow. "This should only take you a few minutes as the application form is short."

"But I cannot get through," wheezed Hectic.

"That does not matter. I can slide the form to you from around the corner. Please fill them out from where you are." Hectic heard a slight rustling, and three pieces of paper slid slowly into his sight.

"I need a pen." There was a slight pause. Then Hectic heard a sound like a pebble rolling, and a pen rolled into the light of the triangle. The ant shadow slid off the triangle of light and the plicking sound resumed.

Hectic suddenly became very angry. *How outrageous! How absurd!* he thought. *Why does the ant treat me in such a ridiculous manner for no apparent reason? Why couldn't the ant at least have him fill out the forms somewhere comfortable, where they could meet face to face? What had he done to deserve such unjust treatment?* He was quite certain he had done nothing and was very tempted to curse at the insect. However, he quickly remembered that he had no points and bated his anger. He had become an unwilling participant in a strange game where the insect was one of the referees. If he did not play according to the insect's rules, he might starve.

rootlet 4.31 — the badger

In his awkward twisted position, Hectic could not get his animal arm free to hold the papers steady while he wrote with his human hand. Consequently, he had considerable trouble writing legibly. "I'm all set," he yelled out when he had completed the application. The plicking stopped, and after a brief pause, the ant shadow re-emerged on the triangle. Hectic feared that the ant would reject his sloppy application and make him fill out another one. However, after a longer pause the ant spoke.

"You are now qualified to work. Go see the badger. He will be waiting for you just outside the double doors."

Hectic was greatly relieved, as he backed out of the awkward position. He made his way out of the funnel, opened the door, and plunged back into the confusion of the chamber. Standing about fifty feet down the ditch was a badger, who was waving Hectic forward. When Hectic got within about ten feet, the badger darted towards Hectic like a pulse of light. He stopped abruptly inches from Hectic's face, and rapidly chittered something that was completely incomprehensible through the noise. After only a few seconds, the badger stopped chittering and scuttled away. He went a few feet before jerking around and vigorously beckoning Hectic to follow him. Hectic had to move as quickly as he could to keep up with the hyper badger. The badger raced up one of the ladder stairs and out of the ditch with Hectic in hot pursuit. They whipped around a disorientating number of corners, ducked under pipes, and weaved in between wires that hung haphazardly into nowhere. The chaos was even more overwhelming without the linear walls of the ditch to help direct Hectic's eyes. In the pulsing lights, the badger looked like a blurry brown blob blinking jarringly in and out of sight.

     As the chase continued, Hectic quickly became exhausted. He wanted to abort the chase, close his beleaguered eyes, and rest his overheated brain. Only his fear of becoming forever lost in the Chamber of Belts kept him chasing after the badger. They raced through an array of different concrete ditches with wildly varying dimensions. Some of the ditches were only a few feet wide but as much as twenty feet deep, while others were about fifty feet wide and only a few feet deep. The badger scuttled through the lengths of each ditch for an indeterminate distance and then unpredictably shot up one of the silvery ladder-stairs. While in a ditch, Hectic was able to focus easier and regain a little energy. Unfortunately, the badger's excursions out of the ditches and into the utterly asphyxiating confusion above were becoming longer. Hectic felt like a sick salmon that was constantly flopping out of a stream and onto the banks.

Finally, the badger came to a long rectangular cabin and stopped. Hectic closed his eyes for just a second. When he opened them, the badger was gone. Hectic looked in the cabin and saw a grizzly bear, a pit bull terrier, and a squirrel. The animals were busy removing packages from a belt that flowed into the cabin, and stacking them neatly along the back wall. Hectic stood watching them and wondered how he would get back to his apartment. The squirrel noticed him, and shook his bushy tail at him in a disapproving manner. Hectic shrugged his shoulders and walked apprehensively towards the squirrel in bewilderment. All three animals looked expectedly at the belt and then at Hectic. Hectic took a package off the belt and looked tentatively at the animals. The animals looked expectedly back at him and then at the stack towards the rear of the cabin. Hectic placed the package neatly on the stack, and the animals nodded affirmatively.

    Hectic realized that his job was to take the packages off the belt and fit them neatly into the cabin. He breathed a sigh of relief that his job was so simple and began to happily work. Just as he was getting in a nice groove, the badger appeared. He led Hectic to a different cabin where he stacked packages with other animals. The badger appeared a short while later, and led Hectic to a third cabin. As the day wore on, Hectic lost count of all the cabins to which the badger had taken him. After a long tiring day of running around and stacking, the badger led Hectic down a set of double-doors at the end of a ditch. With an impatient shove, the badger sent Hectic through the doors and into a hall of silence. Hectic correctly assumed that his workday was over, but he incorrectly assumed he was in the same hall from which he had first entered the CB. When he followed the seemingly familiar hallway, he soon entered an utterly unfamiliar part of The Bowels. He spent several hours wandering through the unrelenting cacophony, before finally finding his way back to his apartment. After he had slammed the front door shut, he collapsed to the floor in an all too familiar state of dizziness. When Hectic recovered his senses a bit, he wondered when he was next supposed to show up for work. He decided that he would go to bed and return to the CB as soon as he awoke. After his sleeping session, he followed the belts down to the CB. Just as before, he walked through a quiet hallway that entered the CB and turned into a ditch.

    Hectic was surprised to see the badger waiting for him in the middle of the ditch. Just like the previous day, the badger led him through the flickering madness from cabin to cabin. At whatever time the workday ended, the badger shoved Hectic out of the CB and into another hallway of silence. The hallway again led Hectic to unfamiliar sections of The Bowels. Hectic had to wander again though the cacophonous madness for hours before he found his apartment. He assumed that as the days passed he would learn to find his way back to his apartment from the CB. Yet, after several days he could still not find his way home. The badger always managed to direct him to different hallways that led somewhere utterly unfamiliar.

rootlet 4.32 — trouble in the CB

He took some comfort in knowing that at least he was performing well at work. Neither the badger, nor any of the other animals had indicated that he was doing anything wrong. Then one day a sneering hyena snatched a package from Hectic that he was just about to add to a stack. In the following days, other animals began to increasingly snatch packages away from him. Hectic began to wonder if he had really been doing a good job after all. He couldn't be sure, because nobody ever said anything to him. He began to worry. Perhaps he was doing a poor job. Perhaps the animals had only left him alone at first, because they viewed him as a trainee. Perhaps they had been growing increasingly impatient with him as the days wore on. What would he do if the badger fired him? He would no longer be able to earn points—he would starve!

Eventually, Hectic figured out that the animals wanted him to pack the boxes more securely together. He tried to be more careful, but the task was more difficult than he would have guessed. The belts were maliciously turning against him and were increasingly delivering their boxes at a more erratic rate. Sometimes individual packages trickled slowly into the cabins. Other times, the belts flooded the cabins with deep rivers of boxes. The sudden surge in boxes often caught Hectic off guard and overwhelmed him. He could not stack them quickly enough, and they would avalanche off the belt onto the floor.

Through the animals' corrective gestures, Hectic learned there were other duties he was supposed to perform that further complicated his job. He was supposed to always place heavy packages on the floor just outside the cabin. A walrus would then shuffle over and lug the heavy package away. All packages labeled HAZARDOUS were supposed to go together just inside the cabin's entrance. Hectic's most difficult duty was ensuring that each box was stacked in the correct cabin. Every box had a five-digit code, which Hectic was supposed to check with a list of codes at the cabin's entrance. If a package's code was not on the list, Hectic was supposed to place the package outside the cabin for the walruses. The walruses would shamble over, flip the packages in their flipper until the code was face side up, and then put the packages in the proper belt.

Checking the boxes' codes gave Hectic more difficulty than his other duties. The boxes often came fast, and the codes were sometimes in small print. Moreover, some of the cabins had very long lists that were not practical to check during sudden surges. Hectic often failed to catch wayward packages. Unfortunately, missing wayward packages angered the badger more than any other mistake. Every time he stacked a package in the wrong cabin, the badger would mysteriously know. He would immediately storm into the cabin and rip the wayward package from the stack. The badger would then thrust the package code face first into Hectic's face and scream incomprehensibly.

Hectic was getting extremely worried about his miserable performance checking packages. If he didn't improve, the badger might fire him. How would he survive? Hectic guessed that he had spent about one hundred days in The Bowels, but he really had no idea. The directions still had not arrived, and he did not know how he could fix the situation. Although he only spent half the day working, he spent the other half wandering through the maze looking for his apartment. When he arrived home, he did not have any energy left to go to the offices and deal with the insects. He had hoped that if he waited long enough, the directions would eventually arrive. He began to consider the terrifying possibility he would never get his directions. The thought resided in his head like a black squid, which was reaching down his throat and squeezing his organs with tentacles of fear. He could be stuck in The Bowels—FOREVER!

rootlet 4.33 — the trouble worsens

The next day when Hectic went to work, he felt especially unhinged. He could not focus on the codes nor could he stack the packages neatly. He began to mutter to himself and insanely hurl the packages towards the back of the cabin, under the delusion that the packages were going to neatly stack themselves. He created a huge jumbled mountain at the back of the cabin that held tenuously together. His delusion dissipated when he heaved a heavy package to the top of the makeshift mountain. The mountain growled like an upset stomach and collapsed into a crashing avalanche. The boxes jounced out of the cabin and crashed onto the floor below. The badger instantly appeared at the entrance of the cabin, put his claws to his head and began screaming. He charged towards Hectic with his fur bristling and his teeth barred. The enraged badger stopped suddenly just short of Hectic and began wildly waving his claw inches from Hectic's face. Hectic was very ashamed and averted his eyes from the badger's scowling face. Instead, he picked a small package on the floor to look at. The badger grabbed Hectic and shook him until spittle oozed from Hectic's mouth. Then he dragged Hectic out of the cabin to the border of the chamber and shoved him through some doors into a hall of silence.

Hectic wandered in the rough direction of his apartment, weeping and muttering softly to himself. Several hours later, he stumbled upon a familiar hallway from which he knew the way home. Yet, his nervous condition did not improve. His thoughts gnawed at each other like a pile of starving rats trapped in a small chamber. He would try to catch one by the tail, but the sickly vermin would slip though his grasp and disappear into the filthy mass. His memories and his conceptions of the future intertwined like vines of madness choking his sanity. The present sensory stimulus of beeping, buzzing, and crawling ants were attacking him like a swarm of bees. His mind could give birth only to fleeting thoughts that squirmed about for a few moments before choking to death in the swirling smoke of emotions.

Hectic had to get back to his apartment where he could be away from the noise! He was not aware that he had begun to run. He jumped over an ant in a natty suit and weaved through a crowd of wandering sheep. "Almost there," he muttered. He was almost to his apartment where he could be away from the continual racket, the sickening crowds of animals, the belts, and utter madness. Arrival. He opened his door, darted inside, and slammed the door shut behind him. "Would he get away from the chaos? Would he find the peace of mind he so desperately needed. NO! NO! NO!" Clutter had progressively taken over his apartment. He could not see the floor through the incredible volumes of paper that the crawling hordes of ants had shoveled in his direction. They exploded in crazy heaps off the top of his desk, peered sadistically from large piles out of his closet. Forms and applications were suffocating everything to death. He could not get away, not get away! They were everywhere he looked. His mind continued to spin and whirl.

"Please," he pleaded with the air. "Please, give me a break. Can I just have one peaceful moment?" The air did not answer. Hectic screamed and began smashing around his apartment in convulsions of rage. He attacked the mounds of forms that lay on the desk, darted to the closet, hurled mounds of forms into the room, kicked them into the air. He yelled at the papers, as he thrashed them with his animal claw and stomped upon the floor. Eventually, Hectic's battle with the papers exhausted him, and he collapsed to the floor where he groaned in agony. As he gulped in the thick air, he watched the forms slip and slide through the air. He waited for them to flutter to the ground, but they did not. Instead, they formed a vortex in the center of the room and began to spin increasingly faster. The vortex intensified into a blinding white tornado that rustled deafeningly loud. Hectic scampered into a corner of the room, covered his head, and trembled. The tornado rumbled with thunder and flashed bolts of lightning. Hectic squeezed himself into a little ball, closed his eyes, and braced himself for an explosion.

ROOT 4.4 — DR. SISYPHUS

The tornado culminated with a loud moist farting noise, emitted a stench of rotting eggs, and then instantly evaporated. Hectic shriveled his nose and uncovered his eyes. In the center of the room was a being comprised entirely of papers. He stood erect on two feet, and looked arrogantly at Hectic.

"Good evening," said the paper thing, "I am Dr. Sisyphus." Hectic, too stunned to say a word, could only stare at the paper being.

"By Jove!" he finally exclaimed. "You're made entirely out of paper forms."

"Of course I am silly. I couldn't exist without them," replied Sisyphus.

"Mr. Sisyphus, is there something—"

"That's Dr. Sisyphus! Now please, I am here to help you. The very least you could do in return is offer me a cup of black."

"Certainty," Hectic responded, "but may I ask you what have you have come for?"

"We will get to that in due time. First, though, I would like my black; and could I have that with two lumps of white?"

Hectic went obediently into the kitchen, and took out one of the many cans of instant black that he had purchased. Increasingly curious as to why the paper thing had come to his apartment, he peeked cautiously into the main room to see what he was doing. Dr. Sisyphus was sitting comfortably on the couch with his right leg crossed over his left leg. He was patiently waiting for his black as he casually flipped his right foot up and down. After Hectic had prepared the black, he brought out a cup for himself and one for the Dr. Sisyphus.

"Thank you," said Sisyphus politely. The Doctor raised the cup to his papery lips and took a long slurpy sip. "Very good black," he said nodding his head approvingly. "You prepare an exceptional cup of black, and the amount of white you added is just right. I thank you."

"You're very welcome," replied Hectic.

A long awkward pause ensued in which Hectic nervously watched Sisyphus slurp his black and flip his foot. Finally, Hectic spoke. "If I could just go back to what I was asking you before, and I don't mean to be rude. Why exactly are you here?"

Sisyphus slowly put his cup of black down, crossed his finger, brought his hands up to his chin, and looked studiously at Hectic.

"I am here to help you," he said with an affected look of concern. I understand that you have had some trouble of late getting yourself organized."

"How did you know?"

"My job is to know. Besides, word gets around in The Bowels."

"You're quite right! I've had considerable trouble," responded Hectic emphatically. "I have found the seemingly simple task of acquiring my directions to be inexplicably difficult. I'm baffled as to why I haven't been able to get them." Hectic paused and furrowed his brow. He was trying to remember when his troubles began, but he could not. His entire life seemed to consist of working at the CB or trying to track down his directions to the top. His existence was like the passageways of The

Bowels—with no beginning and no end. Hectic muttered and stared pensively into space.

"What are you thinking?" Dr. Sisyphus asked.

"I don't know," Hectic said with a sigh. "I just… I just—just can't pull myself together. My work exhausts me, and I have the hardest time finding my way home afterwards. By the time I do get home, I don't have the energy to track down my directions. I go and talk with the ants, but I never seem to fully understand them. Every time I think I am going to receive my directions, some detail or complication prevents them from coming to me."

Hectic sat down on the couch next to Dr. Sisyphus and began to cry. Sisyphus reached over and gently patted Hectic's knee with his papery hand.

"Mr. Norder, is there anything else you want to tell me—anything else at all?"

Hectic took a big breath of air. "Well, I do have a peculiar feeling…. This kind of—"

"Inner chaos?" the doctor interrupted.

"That's exactly right!" Hectic exploded off the couch. "Chaos has entered me and spread throughout my mind. I get exhausted focusing on the boxes at work and trying to comprehend all the forms the ants give me. I have to fight continually to block out the hoards of fleeting images that compete for my mind's attention."

The Doctor nodded his head knowingly, and then resumed slurping his black and flipping his foot in the air. "I know what the problem is," he said. "Your feelings of chaos are typical among animals who are newcomers to The Bowels, although, your chaos has persisted longer than the chaos of most other animals." Dr. Sisyphus tapped a finger on the rim of his cup and gave Hectic a faint crooked smile. "Do you know where you were before you entered The Bowels?" he asked Hectic. Hectic furrowed his brow and again tried to remember.

"I don't know," he said, finally.

Dr. Sisyphus got up with a rustling sound and crossed his arms in the air as if resting them on an invisible podium. He conspicuously cleared his throat, and began to speak in an intellectual tone. As he orated, he rested his chin in one hand and gestured majestically with the other.

"You came from a place called Nature, which essentially is chaos. Nature is crude, and breeds the worst habits into her offspring. Nature's offspring are all uncivilized, savage, and disorderly. When they come into The Bowels, they are unable to think or act properly. Frankly, I find their behavior very disturbing. However, I have committed myself to instilling order in the disorderly offspring of nature. As you have learned for yourself, happiness is not compatible with chaos. In fact, happiness is order. I have come to direct you towards the happiness you richly deserve."

Sisyphus then abruptly sat back down on the couch, where he resumed his cup slurping and foot flipping. He sat, and looked at Hectic with his slight papery smile for an awkwardly long time. Finally, Hectic lost his patience.

"Damn you!" he yelled. "Just tell me what I need to—"

Dr. Sisyphus sprang of the couch, and to Hectic's amazement, thrust his arm into his own stomach. He violently rustled around his insides before tearing out a large rectangular object, which he tossed in front of Hectic's feet. Sisyphus pointed at the object with a papery finger and said, "Inside this textbook you will find all the information you need to get to the top. If you have any question, come see me at my office. Do you have a writing implement? I want you to write down my office hours. No, no, no. Don't bother looking for one," he said as Hectic began searching around the apartment. "I've got one." Sisyphus stuck two fingers into his ear, and slowly pulled forth a pen. He handed the pen to Hectic and said, "You can keep this one. I see you have plenty of paper to write on, so here is my schedule. I'm in Sector 9, Quadrant 43, Sector PQ you can stop by at..." and then he recited a long list of erratically varying times. After he finished speaking, he abruptly dashed out of the apartment into the never-ending confusion.

Hectic picked up the mammoth tome and looked at the front cover. The title was *The Bowels: An Equal Opportunity Structure.* There was also a picture of various animals in shiny black pants and white shirts. They were standing joyously in a long line, as an ant handed them forms from behind a counter.

He realized that he would need quite a bit of time to read the text. Nevertheless, he felt encouraged. The book *The Bowels* at least had a beginning and end, which was a large improvement over The Bowels in which he lived. With some persistence, he could read the book cover to cover and glean all the information contained within the pages. However, he was too exhausted at that point to do anything. He needed to get some sleep and then find out if he still had a job before he did any reading. Hectic put the book down on the floor and went to bed.

rootlet 4.41 — <u>THE BOWELS</u>

As was his usual routine upon waking, Hectic trudged nervously off to the land of the belts. When he exited a hall of silence into the chamber, the badger was waiting for him down the ditch. The badger auspiciously did not act any differently than all the other times Hectic had arrived. Hectic actually found relief participating in the wild chase that initiated each workday. They did the typical route down numerous ditches, up various ladder-stairs, under a myriad of tangled pipes, and to a cabin. Hectic immediately noticed that animals were not loading packages from the belt into the cabin. Instead, they were unloading packages from the cabin onto the belt, which pumped the boxes away. Hectic hopped into the cabin and began working with the animals to unload the boxes. He assumed that the badger had mercifully transferred him to the unloading sector instead of firing him, because he found unloading far easier than loading. He no longer had to worry about stacking the packages neatly or checking the codes. For the next few days, Hectic unloaded the boxes without any problems. The badger, as he had before, came at random intervals and whisked him away to other cabins.

As before, no one ever took Hectic somewhere quiet and explained to him exactly what his job description was. He assumed that there was some aspect of his new task that he was performing incorrectly, and he fully anticipated the animals would eventually begin their corrective gesturing. Two weeks later, his fellow unloaders did indeed begin angrily gesturing at him. Their behavior had become familiar to Hectic and did not disconcert him. He patiently watched the agitated animals' gestures and modified his performance until they seemed satisfied. He managed to correct all his errors within two days and completely free himself from the animal's constant nagging.

His work situation had greatly improved. Yet, He was still having trouble finding his way home. The badger still consistently managed to bring him to unfamiliar halls, which seemed unlimited in number. Hectic was more intent than ever to get home early, because he wanted time to study *The Bowels*.

The day he began reading the book and saw that the voluminous writing was an explanation of how the offices worked, he was elated. He believed that he would soon master the secret logic of the ants and track down a copy of his directions. Even better, he might learn where the ants kept the original copy. Then, he could go directly to the source and reduce his interactions with the niggling insects.

Every day after finding his way home, Hectic would eagerly read the text. His enthusiasm slowly fizzled, however, as time tortuously oozed forward without him learning anything. He discovered that *The Bowels* was every bit as convoluted as The Bowels in which he lived. He spent less time traipsing through the twisted hallways of the bowels looking for his directions and more time traipsing through the twisted sentences of *The Bowels* looking for directions to his directions. Dr. Sisyphus's prose was drier than a hundred loaves of stale bread. Hectic tried to force himself to read, but the words lodged in his mind's throat. His eyes blinked continuously as if they were chewing each word ten times. Despite his best efforts, *The Bowels* remained as indigestible as ever. As he choked on his boredom, he wondered angrily why Dr. Sisyphus had written such a dreadfully tedious book. Hectic knew that if the prose were more interesting, he would have finished the book a long time ago. Perhaps, he would already be enjoying himself at the place to which the directions would take him. On one particularly frustrating read, Hectic began to curse Dr. Sisyphus. "Damn you Sisyphus!" he bellowed. "If I were to write one of these so called books, I would at least make an attempt to hold the attention of the reader." Hectic stopped for a second and thought about what he had just said. He began to laugh for the first time in a while, because the mere idea of him writing anything in all the chaos was utterly ridiculous.

    A few days after he had cursed Sisyphus, Hectic stumbled upon a small picture of a hexagonal framework imbedded deep within the textual labyrinth. Hectic had not seen any pictures in the book before and was immediately curious what the framework was. As he read that page, the information seemed to rise from the book like a tidal wave and flood him with excitement. The framework was the Chamber of Directions, which apparently had the directions for every animal on file. When Hectic read that the CD was just at the end of the Upward62 Tunnel LB, he began jumping for joy. He knew exactly where that tunnel was. He dashed out of his apartment and took the sideward left-bound pass to Chamber 178. Hectic crossed over the 178 and entered the Upward62. The 62 was a perfectly round tunnel that initially extended straight ahead. As Hectic continued, the tunnel began to gradually angle upward and become increasingly smaller like an elephant trunk reaching for leaves. Towards the end, the Saco was only a few feet wide and extended straight up. Hectic had to strain his body against the inner confines of the tunnel, and inch upward in fits and starts. He mustered all his strength and struggled out of the tunnel into a drafty, well-lit chamber

rootlet 4.42 — the chamber of directions

Hectic closed his eyes and lay wheezing with exhaustion by the edge of the tunnel's exit. As he was recovering his breath, he noticed that the chamber seemed to be wheezing along with him. He opened his eyes and got up. The chamber was the largest he could remember seeing, for the ceilings and walls seemed to be miles away. Hundreds of neatly dressed, paper-carrying ants scurried to and from the entrance of a walkway about one hundred feet from Hectic. The walkway ascended upon a series of increasingly higher arches towards a mountainous hexagonal framework, which Hectic assumed was the main entranceway leading into the main chamber, and then to the various departments and sub-departments.

The framework was an intricate pattern of vastly varied-sized hexagons in which the smaller hexagons arranged repeatedly into larger hexagons. The ants entered and exited the framework through an opening high up on the structure via the ascending walkway.

Suddenly, the framework began to contract— and with a loud wheezing noise expelled a blast of warm dank air into Hectic's face. The framework then expanded— and a cool breeze hit Hectic on the back. The structure was contracting and swelling like a heaving chest. With each breath, the hexagon shapes expanded and constricted like thousands of mouths gasping for air. During the framework's heaving, the walkways amazingly did not move. The ants continued their march seemingly indifferent to the motion around them.

Hectic was baffled, for the text had not mentioned that the building moved. He decided to check if he was at the right building with one of the ants. "Excuse me sir," he said to a slow-moving ant that was coming towards him down the walkway. "Is that moving building the Chamber of Directions?" The ant released a stack of papers from his mandibles, stood up on his two hind legs, and put his front legs over Hectic's shoulders. The ant's left eye was a prune-like concavity of dead desiccated tissue, and his right middle leg was missing. He tilted his head to the left head and observed Hectic with his good right eye.

"Sure is," the ant said. "Are you looking for your directions?"

"Yes, but I am afraid to enter a building that moves so drastically. Have the contracting bars ever crushed anyone before? Does anyone ever lose their balance and fall?"

"Your fear is unfounded good sir. I have worked at the CD for over thirty years, and I have never seen anyone get hurt in there. If you would like, I can probably tell you precisely where your files are. What is your name?"

"Hectic Norder," said Hectic.

"Hmmm… Norder… Sounds familiar," said the ant reflectively. "Now let me think. Oh yes, I remember seeing your file. Your directions should be on the fourteenth floor in file 103072."

"But which department, which room?" asked Hectic.

"There are no departments," the ant replied. "The whole building is comprised of one department if you will. Yes, one huge accumulation of file upon file upon files."

Hectic hesitated for a second and then asked, "What happened to your eye and leg?"

"I'm not sure," said the ant. "I think I was born that way." The ant then promptly got off Hectic and crawled away.

Hectic walked to the walkway and began the ascent up. When he arrived at the entrance of the CD, he stopped and peered through the matrix. Through the shifting bars, he could see the ants marching up and into the framework upon the winding walkway. Hectic carefully watched the walkway through several cycles of the framework's breathing. The walkway never shifted and none of the ants ever lost their balance and fell.

Hectic finally took a deep breath and with great trepidation joined the stream of paper-carrying ants entering the CD. The framework contracted around him and a warm breeze blew into his face. As He continued to climb up the winding walkway, he began to relax, for the walkway never moved, nor did the shifting bars encroach into the space above the walkway. Farther up, a row of numerically ordered file cabinets began on the left side of the walkway. 451-460, 461-470, 471-480— the numbers on the file cabinets got higher as he ascended up into the CD. Hectic still had a long way to go before he reached 103072.

The walkway led him deeper into the honeycomb matrix where the number of ants had dwindled. At that juncture, the intensity of the light oscillated with each breath of the honeycomb. With each inhalation, the framework densified and dimmed the light; while with each exhalation, the network rarefied and bright light illuminated the walkway.

"99,971-99,980, 99,981-99,990—" The files ended and the walkway dipped sharply down into some shadows. Hectic peered down into the dip and could just make out that the walkway melded into a long rectangular piebald strip. He waited for his eyes to adjust to the dimmer light and looked more carefully. He observed that the strip stretched and contracted in conjunction with the frameworks breathing.

Hectic edged cautiously down into the shadows. At a closer distance, he could just make out that the strip was actually a section of the walkway thickly covered in ants. The black and white of the ants' suits is what made the walkway a piebald appearance from a distance. The swarm was restricted to a short strip on the other side of the dip where the walkway curved sharply upward. *Why were the ants swarming on that specific section of the walkway and nowhere else?* he wondered. He trembled and edged forward. He was leery about crossing through the swarm of ants, but the strip was short. He would only have to negotiate through the swarm for a minute or two, and then he would be on the upper walkway.

As he edged closer, the framework exhaled and brief darkness ensued. Hectic advanced to the very edge of the swarm and waited for the dim light to reappear before he took another step. The structure creaked, the framework inhaled, and the light effused dimly through the matrix. Hectic looked down to carefully place his first step and recoiled with terror. The ants were not swarming over the ascending strip as he had thought: They were themselves the ascending strip.

They had interlinked together with their powerful mandibles to bridge a gap in the walkway. In the seething meshwork, Hectic could not tell where one ant's body started and another ended. They seemed to blend into a writhing blanket of spindly legs, mandibles, white shirts, and black pants.

Hectic looked to see if there was another way he could cross the chasm. There was not—only the ant bridge. If he were to cross the chasm without using the ant bridge, he would have to climb through the shifting bars. The matrix of bars only extended across the chasm far below the ant bridge. Hectic would have to climb several hundred feet just to get to the upper walkway. In all likelihood, the bars would crush him during one of the CD's exhalations. The ant bridge, on the other hand, was only about fifty feet.

As Hectic was thinking about what to do, a few ants marched down from the upper walkway and perfunctorily crossed over their interlocking brothers. Hectic watched for a while and witnessed several other ants cross over their brothers without the slightest hint of trouble. He soon concluded that the ant bridge was sturdy and his only viable option to get to the upper walkway. He took a deep breath, waited for the light of an inhalation, and courageously stepped onto an insect's head.

The bridge shifted with the building's breathing, and Hectic quickly got down on all fours to maintain his balance. He grabbed onto various shirt collars and pant legs as he crawled slowly upwards. The ants occasionally rubbed an antenna against his face or a mandible against his chin, but did not hinder his advance.

Hectic had negotiated most of the ant bridge, when a sudden surge of ants came swarming towards him from the upper level. Instead of veering around him, they clambered over him and pushed him down into the bridge. The interlinking ants quickly clamped onto his limbs, and incorporated him into the bridge. Hectic screamed as a pair of mandibles dug into the flesh of his sensitive human wrist. The structure inhaled, and he stretched out like an X. As the weak light filtered in, he saw that he was suspended thousands of feet in the air. Between him and the ground, the hexagons opened and closed like carnivorous jaws hungrily waiting for falling prey. Hectic roared and ripped his bear-arm out of a pair of mandibles. He used his powerful claw to pull himself back onto the ant-bridge and scrambled up onto the upper walkway.

An interlinking ant, who had tried to hold onto Hectic, lost his balance and fell. He bounced violently halfway down through the framework before catching a bar in the middle of his body. He remained draped over the bar until a hexagonal mouth closed on his midsection and severed his abdomen. The truncated ant jounced the rest of the way through the framework until finally landing on the ground. The insect schlepped away dragging his thorax, which oozed a trail of goo on the ground behind him.

The walkway above the ant-bridge was as dim as the shadowy dip from which Hectic had just come. He had to wait for an inhalation to see that the files started at 100,001-100,010. Hectic shook with excitement, for he realized he was very close to his file. He wanted to progress quicker, but was afraid he might fall of the walkway. He walked quickly when there was light, but cautiously stopped when the building exhaled and utter darkness fell.

Finally, he arrived at file cabinet 103,070-103,080. At that point, he was in almost constant darkness. He could only see for a split second at the very climax of each inhalation. The window of sight was to brief for Hectic to be positive he was at the right file cabinet with only one glimpse. He observed the cabinet through two more inhalations. After the third blink of light had passed, he was satisfied he was looking at the correct cabinet. Hectic decided he could open the drawer in the dark and search for his directions during the blinks of light. He reached out into the darkness and successfully grasped the handle with his human hand. He pulled, but the drawer did not open; he pulled harder, but the drawer still did not open.

Perhaps after finally finding the cabinet, he would not be able to simply open the drawer. A sense of injustice, fear, and frustration flooded him. Hectic suddenly had the impression that he was in the center of an amphitheater. Chaos in a hodgepodge of forms filled every seat and watched his misery with pleasure.

Hectic roared in rage and lashed out with his bear claw to pull the handle. The drawer ripped loose, and Hectic stumbled backwards over the walkway. As he smashed down through countless bars, he somehow managed to keep a grasp on the drawer. He fortunately landed on the walkway, which happened to circle underneath.

Miraculously, Hectic was not badly hurt. Despite the terrifying fall he had just endured, he could think only of his directions. He rolled over and peaked into the dislodged drawer. Laced into the inside of the drawer with white silky strands was a small white oval object. The skin on the oval cracked, and a small white ant burst out of the oval. As the nascent ant scurried over Hectic's body and out of sight, he could sense chaos watching him from every seat in the amphitheater. The chaos manifests snickered at him through malformed jaws and slapped their deformed hands against their knobby knees with glee.

rootlet 4.43 — the end of Dr. Sisyphus

Homicidal rage flooded Hectic. He had to kill somebody, and Dr. Sisyphus just happened to pop into his mind. He shot up and stormed towards the Doctor's office. Hectic did not remember what the Doctor's office hours were, but he did not care. If the Doctor was in, he would kill him immediately. If not, he would wait outside his door and kill him when he arrived.

As Hectic continued on his hurricane path, he envisioned Dr. Sisyphus sitting in a special reserved section of the amphitheater of chaos. An entourage of servile ants was bringing him cups of black with white cubes. The Dr. was slurping his black, flipping his foot, and taking great pleasure in Hectic's misery. He was the papery god— the author who had penned Hectic's torturous existence. He was the one who scrambled

Hectic's thoughts and denied him even a moment's peace. The text *The Bowels* was only a tiny chapter in a much larger book of futility and hopelessness.

When Hectic arrived at the office, Dr. Sisyphus was there. He was sitting behind a desk that faced the entranceway causally flipping his foot in the air as he perused over some forms. He immediately saw Hectic and gave him a courteous smile.

"Oh. Hello Mr. Norder. Do you have a question for me regarding the text?" he asked amicably. Dr. Sisyphus' polite behavior did not square with the nefarious image of him that had just sprouted in Hectic's mind. The disparity nonplussed Hectic who began to mumble nervously. Dr. Sisyphus put his coffee down on the desk and firmly planted both feet on the ground.

"Mr. Norder, what is wrong?" asked the Doctor. "Is there something I can do for you?"

"Your text is completely absurd," blurted Hectic, "just like everything else in this place!"

The Dr's jaw dropped. "Hectic my boy!" he exclaimed. "*The Bowels* is one of the finest books you will ever find. I'm sure you just misunderstood something."

Hectic's confusion quickly reorganized back into rage. "One of the finest!" he spat. "Your book is convoluted, unfathomable, and worse of all—utterly boring! Furthermore, the one part I understood turned out to be false. On one page, you describe the alleged Chamber of Directions where all the directions to the top are stored. Well, I just came from the CD. When I looked in the file in which my directions were supposed to be, I found nothing but a giant ant egg."

Dr. Sisyphus stood up and bent forward until his chest hit the top of his desk with a crumpling sound. He reached back between his legs and thrust his hand into his hind end. He rustled around his innards for a few seconds before pulling out a gigantic book, which he slammed on the table with a violent thump. The title of Dr. Sisyphus's latest offering was *The Bowels 2: The Next Movement in Interoffice Organization*."

Sisyphus stood up straight and looked proudly at his book. "Mr. Norder, don't be distressed. If my first book didn't help you, my second book surely will," he said confidently.

Hectic furrowed his brows and began flipping through the book. "On what page does *The Bowels 2* tell me the way to the top?" he asked pointedly.

Sisyphus scrunched his face with such confusion that the papery skin around his eyes made a crumpling sound. Suddenly, he perked up as if experiencing a great epiphany.

"Oh!" he exclaimed. "Now I see the source of your frustration. You thought my book was supposed to actually show you how to get to the top. Oh you poor, silly, confused, creature. Let me clarify. I do not write of the actual Bowels. I write only of hypothetical bowels. The intent of my writing is to help creatures think in an ordered way. You especially should benefit from my writing, for you are an especially disorganized thinker. If you continue to read my books diligently, your thinking will organize. Eventually, you will have the capacity to organize your affairs and find your directions. Of course, once you think in an ordered way you will not want to leave The Bowels. After all, you can subsist here perfectly fine. Why would any rational mind want to leave and go somewhere that is potentially unsafe?"

Hectic realized he should have been outraged, but instead he felt strangely calm and clearheaded. "If reading your book makes me want to stay here, I don't want to read one more word. Subsisting is not enough for me; I want to live." Hectic looked the Dr. firmly in the eye and said, "I respectfully request that you simply tell me the actual way out of the actual Bowels. Please show me the way out of certain subsistence and into possible danger."

Hectic's forward request outraged the doctor. He shook with anger and leaned menacingly over the desk.

"I don't know the way through The Bowels. Even if I did, I wouldn't tell you," he snarled. "The mere fact that you ask me directly for your directions demonstrates to me that you are completely incorrigible. Congratulations Mr. Norder," spat Sisyphus. "You are the first creature I know of that is beyond my help."

At that precise moment, all the frustration and anger accumulating inside Hectic boiled over like a volcano, pouring forth violent red lava. Hectic lunged over the desk, caught Dr. Sisyphus behind the head with his bear arm, and slammed the doctor's face into the desk. As he held the doctor down, he maneuvered to Sisyphus' side of the desk. He continued to hold Sisyphus— who was futilely thrashing about under Hectic's powerful claw— bent over the desk. Dr. Sisyphus began to cry out, but Hectic crumpled his face against the desk and muffled his mouth.

"What's that you are saying?" mocked Hectic. "What? Speak up. I can't hear you. Oh, you want me to return your book to you immediately. Well, okay!"

Hectic picked up the massive text and carefully aligned a corner with Sisyphus' hind end. Sisyphus began to struggle more ferociously and kicked his legs up. "Now, don't be impatient Dr." said Hectic. "How am I supposed to return the book, if you wriggle around like that?" Hectic stretched one of his orangutan legs behind the Dr. and pinned his papery legs to the desk drawers. He realigned the book and began the returning process with a vigorous shove. He got the book deep enough into the orifice that the title <u>The Bowels</u> appeared to be *owels*. Yet, he could not get the two distant corners of the book through the back way and complete the return. He was simply not at a good angle to sufficiently direct his force. He swiftly let go of the Dr's head, braced his back against the back wall, and delivered a sharp kick to the book before the Dr. could react. The book and Hectic's hoof sunk deep into Sisyphus' backside. The papery coils of the Dr's intestinal tract entangled and snared Hectic's hoof. Hectic hoped up and down on his free hoof straining to maintain balance. He finally managed to lean forward and clutch the Dr's buttocks for support. He pushed against the buttocks with all his might. There was a tearing noise—and Hectic's hoof came out in a tangle of papery intestines. Hectic did not bother to disentangle his hoof; he simply left the office. The tangle on his hoof was still connected to the Dr. via a few strands. As he walked away, the Dr. unraveled. Soon, all that was left of Sisyphus was a long coil of paper that threaded half the distance from the Dr's office to Hectic's apartment.

ROOT 4.5 — RED RAGE

The period following Dr. Sisyphus' unraveling could have been a few days, or many months. For now that Hectic had no hope, he was numb. With a blank look etched upon his face, he walked lifelessly amongst the masses. No plan of action drove him from one place to another, and no goal beckoned him to move. His movement was as purposeless as the twitching muscle fibers of an animal just after decapitation. His unconscious wandering only an accidental by-product of a physiologically predisposition to walk

"How did I get here?" Hectic became aware that he was at the Chamber of Belts. He surmised he had been in a trance like state. Inexplicably, the trance he had apparently been in had just abruptly ended. His mind began to whir with questions in an attempt to make order out of his fragmented consciousness. *Had habit delivered him here? When was the last time he had been here?* His attempts to establish a time line for himself were utterly futile. For all he knew, he could have been coming to the Chamber

of Belts every day. On the other hand, his sudden awakening could have been the first time he had been to the belts for several months.

He was somewhere in the chamber where an unusually dense tangle of belts converged above him. From a distance, Hectic saw a hog riding a package towards him down one of the belts. The hog saw Hectic and began gesturing wildly and shaking his head disapprovingly. More animals came riding packages down the belts towards Hectic. When they saw him, they also began gesturing disapprovingly at him. "What do you want?" Hectic yelled. With all the noise, Hectic could not even hear his own voice. The animals seemed oblivious to the fact that he was trying to communicate with them.

The light in the chamber began to flicker and turned blood red. The hellish light darkened the animal's facial cavities and made them look like demons. Their eyes and mouths were dark red as if oozing the blood of rage. In the midst of all the red chaos and demonic animals, Hectic perceived an ambiguous image drawing closer to him. The image suddenly clarified and Hectic saw an ant in spiffy attire crawling upside down on a pipe. Hectic turned away in disgust and nearly bumped into the badger who was suddenly right behind him. The badger had the same demonic bloody look as the other animals and began furiously waving his claw in Hectic's face.

"What are you saying?" Hectic yelled. "What do you want? What am I supposed to do?" The redness seemed to wash over Hectic and flood him with rage. He felt as if he was floating up above the badger, as if he was a black cloud hovering amongst the pipes and belts. From up above, he felt his mismatched arms reaching down towards the badger. They looked incredibly long and thin like two stalks of bamboo. He watched his human hand and bear claw clutch the badger's neck far down below. The badger's eyes bulged out of his furry face, as if they were trying to take in the air that his mouth could not. Hectic watched his hand and claw continue to clutch the neck. The badger's head flopped about like a fish out of water, and his tongue flailed like an eel. Hectic wondered if the badger was going to die. Then, his hand and claw let go of the neck. The wave of red rage washed Hectic out of the chamber and into one of the quiet hallways.

The next thing he knew, he was at the entrance of his apartment. He tried to remember his walk home, but could not.

Again, his mind tried feverishly to piece together a timeline of where he had been. The only image his mind could retrieve was that of the spiffy ant crawling upside down on the pipe. He could not determine if he had seen that ant hours ago, or months ago. All Hectic knew for sure was that he was very tired. He entered his apartment and immediately went to bed.

ROOT 4.6 — THE HYDRA

As Hectic drifted to sleep, the shadows of his apartment seemed to melt into a stream of dark water. He felt his bed rise and float gently out of his apartment. As he drifted, his mind emptied of all thought and emotion. Then, a warm comforting sensation filled the emptiness. He heard a beautiful gurgling noise, and opened his eyes. He was lying next to a stream with clear water that ran as smoothly as a daydream between two structured banks. He looked up at the friendly yellow eye in the innocent blue sky, and he felt warmth stream down upon him. Only a little black dot marred the face of blue like a tiny scar. He assumed the dot was a bird flying at a distance, but he could not be quite sure. As he looked, the dot began to grow bigger and spread tiny tendrils into the blue like a parasite of the sky.

A sudden hissing distracted him from the sky and pulled his attention to the stream. The water had stopped gurgling and was releasing great multitudes of tiny bubbles. Hectic turned away in fear only to face the thing in the sky. The dot had grown into the vague black image of a giant jellyfish with long thin tendrils that reached out and stung the blue. The sound of angry boiling jerked his attention back towards the stream. The bubbling had exponentially intensified and the stream was violently boiling. Hectic looked back up towards the sun and begged for mercy, but black clouds had formed and obscured the sun. The clouds began whipping across the sky in a desperate race to nowhere, and the banks of the stream constricted. The seething water turned reddish-black, and whirled around in futile circles. "Madness!" screamed Hectic. The water exploded into swirling red flames, and from the center of the vortex came a horrible cacophony of noises.

From the eye of the maelstrom slithered forth a massive three-headed serpent with two gargantuan gorilla arms and wearing a starchy white shirt with numerous pockets. All the pockets had pocket protectors with gigantic blue pens clipped over them. The heads screamed and moaned in a horrendous hurly-burly that overwhelmed Hectic. The inchoate sounds picked apart his sanity like hundreds of vultures upon a decaying corpse. For a few fleeting seconds, Hectic thought he could almost discern a word that one of the heads would utter. However, the near discernment only intensified his madness. For neither could he dismiss the serpent's noise as a giant blur, nor could he really listen to what the serpent was saying. Although he could not be certain, he had the impression that at least one head was enraged. The serpent seemed to be spitting vile words from one of his mouths as if they were putrid tasting. Another head seemed to be wailing like a mother that had suffered the loss of all her children. The third head seemed to moan and groan as if what he always wanted in life was constantly dangling just out of his reach.

    The heads twisted around each other in such erratic motions, that Hectic could not discern which head was doing what. He was not even certain if they were doing in general what he thought they were doing. The huge gorilla arms with their beefy fingers flailed about and gestured erratically. For a few fleeting seconds, he had the impression that the hands were pointing accusingly. Other times, he thought the hands faced upward as if begging for mercy. However, the serpent moved with such herky-jerky motions that Hectic could not tell. The chaos was tearing him apart.

Hectic tried to look away and escape the torture. Instantly, the serpents shot sticky red strands from the tip of his tail that covered Hectic and rooted him in place. Hectic tried to cover his ears, but the strands were pinning his arms to his sides. He tried to close his eyes, but his eyelids were stuck open.

The swooning, wailing, screaming, yelling, groaning, moaning, mumbling serpent slithered closer to Hectic. A chaos of stenches wafted from the beast into Hectic's nose. Through the madness, Hectic thought for a second he could smell rotting flesh and dung. However, the stenches flickered on the edge of existence with such speed that he was not sure what he smelled.

The serpent slithered closer until his starchy white shirt scraped against Hectic's head. The scraping shirt caused a cacophonous cascade of horrid sensations on his skin. He thought, perhaps, parasitic worms were burrowing into his skin and rotting frogs were squishing against him. However, the tactile tornado spun so fast that he could not be sure.

If Hectic's beleaguered brain could have formed thoughts at that moment, he would have wished for death. *Why won't the serpent be merciful and rip me to pieces?* Suddenly, the three heads looked to the sky and screamed in unison. The serpent and the strands around Hectic dissolved into smoke and evaporated. The chaos was gone, and Hectic had survived. He looked up, and saw that the sky had become emblazoned with psychedelic whorls. In the center of the arabesque pattern was a black-bug like shape.

All was silent except the gentle sound of the water gurgling freely between the two ordered banks. Hectic waded into the stream and stretched himself towards the sun. He felt the glorious intermingling of cool wet on his legs, and dry heat on his torso. He took a deep breath and closed his eyes.

ROOT 4.7 —THE LIGHT TO THE TOP

When Hectic opened his eyes, he found himself lying in his bed. Although he was still deep within The Bowels, he felt as if the warmth of the sun had not left him. He could sense the rays passing through the thick walls, the belts, the insects, and onto him. He reached his mismatched arms up towards the top of The Bowels. He could feel the warmth pulling him through the never-ending forms, the wandering animals, and confusion. He was certain that the luminous sun was showing him the way out of The Bowels. He got out of bed and opened his apartment door. A yellow streak of light shone down through the herds of animals marching upon the never-ending hallways. As soon as the light shone upon Hectic, he felt completely at peace. The chaos melted into the distance like the dark background of a painting that makes the light even more visible.

Hectic headed toward the light with the singular focus a salmon exhibits when swimming upstream to spawn. He seemed to know which walkways to take, as if he could see no others. He continued upward through the steady stream of animals that were marching down past him. The currents of animals crashing down upon him were growing stronger, but did not thwart his upward journey. The crowded walkways that Hectic traveled upon ended one after the other, but he always leapt to another and continued on his journey. The light grew even more intensely beautiful. Soon he would escape the flickering lights, tormenting noises, and confusion. Only light filled Hectic's mind. He was getting close- so very close.

OFFSHOOT FIVE
HECTIC MEETS INCHOATE

ROOT 5.1 — THE SWIM

Suddenly, Hectic was underwater. He looked up and saw the refracted image of the sun shining through the water. Hectic coordinated his motley anatomy into a modified breaststroke and swam toward the light. His smaller human arm moved quickly in full circles, while his larger clawed arm moved slower in half circles. As his powerful orangutan legs snapped their hooves together in forceful frog kicks, his arms shot above his head for another stroke. The water swirled and churned over the increased surface area on Hectic's hybrid head where his three inchoate heads had not yet fused. He propelled himself with such energy, however, that even the drag of his grotesque head did not significantly hinder his swift ascent. The water's surface was farther away than Hectic had initially imagined, for he had swum for what seemed like a mile. He was running out of air, but he was confident he would get to the surface. Hectic ascended into an area close to the surface where the sun's rays penetrated the water and extended downward like the columns of an athenaeum. He surged through these columns of light and burst through the water's surface. Immediately, he lost consciousness.

ROOT 5.2 — INCHOATE REGURGITATES HECTIC

In the form of Mandelbrot, Inchoate coughed up Hectic and then began to transform back into his original form. He realized that Hectic would regain consciousness faster than he could return to Inchoate, and didn't want Hectic to see him mid-transformation. As soon as His roots became legs, he hurried away from Hectic as fast as his still transforming body would allow.

He had left Hectic lying on a plateau with a cloudless sky of gold. Yellow columns extended from the sky and penetrated the rich black soil, and grapevines wound up the columns from the soil to the gold above. The grapes on the vines were as big as cantaloupes, and the leaves were great green blankets. Beyond the vineyard, Inchoate stopped at an olive tree and began to sing.

Hectic awoke to the most beautiful sound he had ever heard. Entranced, he began to walk through the vineyard toward the source of that sound. As he got closer, he realized he was listening to someone singing. He could not tell if the lyrics were words or simply vocalizations, for the intonations blended together as if a chorus of canyons was singing in resonating echoes. Hectic felt chaos and order harmonize within him like a double helix of twisted vines winding up a pole. Perhaps for the first time, he experienced total consciousness without suffering. He moved effortlessly and swiftly towards the source of the singing as if he was riding on a stream. Soon, he flowed out of the vineyard and to a small open space in the center of which grew an olive tree.

Underneath the tree Hectic saw Inchoate. His body was dark and wavering like the shadows cast from the moon upon flowing water, and his internal organs were visible through his translucent but swiftly darkening body. Inchoate's huge wolfhead was completely developed with a majestic gray mane tinted with white. Inchoate was moving his jaw as if he was singing, but this was just a mime's act to prevent Hectic from feeling even the slightest anxiety. Inchoate actually produced sound by imperceptibly vibrating his entire body. Far from being a whimsy, Inchoate's singing was part of an epic plan that stemmed from his latest rebirth.

ROOT 5.3 — INCHOATE'S LATEST REBIRTH

Inchoate was a shapeshifter. He was originally born many millennia ago, but even he wasn't exactly sure when. Since his first birth, he had been reborn innumerable times. His births only occurred around moments of intense chaos and during epochs of major transition. Inchoate was always born cunning and sagacious, but these personality traits always had minor variations that resulted from the particular dynamic of his latest rebirth. His most recent birth occurred in the Gulf of Mexico during the twenty-first century.

In the early twenty-first century, Oil exploration had moved to the ocean. On one exploratory rig, there had been a terrible accident. Natural gas flared up the pipes from the ocean floor and exploded onto the platform. The fireball killed eleven men. The rig continued to burn and eventually sank into the sea. There had been an office on that rig that had belonged to a big game hunter. On the walls of his office, the hunter had mounted the heads of all his kills. During the explosion, his office shattered. One of his trophies—a wolf's head—flew through the air and landed in the gulf. For many days, the head drifted with the Gulf Stream.

Underneath where the rig had been, oil gushed from the sea floor into the ocean. Eventually, the oil drifted to the surface and rapidly spread outwards in a toxic sheen. Soon the sheen reached Wolfhead and saturated his fur. He slowly began to sink, but then smoke began to emanate from his mouth. The smoke sank from his mouth like cold vapor, diffused into the water and bubbled underneath him. Wolfhead's glassy eyes softened and his nose began to wriggle. A growl escaped his lips and the water around him immediately turned gray. Wolfhead howled, and the gray water began to spin around him in a tremendous vortex.

The vortex pulled an array of substances and objects that had been floating in the gulf. Bits of human flesh from the explosion, and the organs from dead oil-smothered dolphins sped toward him from many miles away. These bodily remnants spun underneath him within a pillar of oily water. From this sphere, tentacles of black wafted out. These tentacles lightened into gray and became more like animal limbs. Soon, the limbs clarified further into a cross between human arms and wolf legs. The hybrid limbs bent akimbo and touched the spinning sphere. Like a master potter, the handpaws carefully began to constrict and shape the sphere. They elongated the sphere upward from the ocean into a column with Wolfhead resting on top. The centrifugal force within the attenuating column increased and liquids began to separate out from the heart and brain matter. Those liquids infused through Inchoate's latest embodiment and marked his personality with a special trait. This trait was an intense desire to see the world diversify from oil to more environmentally friendly forms of energy.

    Now a good ten feet above the ocean, Wolfhead stopped howling and opened his jaws wide. Smoke bellowed out and engulfed the column of water. He inhaled mightily and sucked in all of the smoke. In the space where the column had been, Inchoate stood fully formed upon the water. He looked disdainfully at the fouled gulf. At the horizon, his keen eyes saw a vessel approaching him from many miles away.

    Inchoate snarled. He had formed with a cynical view of human nature, so he did not want the humans to see him. He believed that they would capture him and exploit him for money. He imagined that they would probably sell him to the circus, and he envisioned people paying good money to see him in a silly suit doing silly tricks alongside trained elephants and half-tame tigers. Inchoate exhaled smoke and transformed himself into a turkey vulture. Quickly, he flew away from the boat and towards the western horizon. After many days of gliding upon thermals, Inchoate came to the plateau where he would regurgitate Hectic several years later

Over the last few years, he had been endeavoring to end the world's oil addiction. He knew the cure; that was not the problem. The real challenge was disseminating his ideas to a chaotic world filled with untrustworthy people. Inchoate concluded that for his dissemination to work, he needed a person with a relentless nature and the wisdom not to force their will upon others. He wanted, in particular, someone who would value opposing views as a means to express and enhance his own ideas. He wanted a gadfly—someone who would spark controversy and trick people into learning about the world's oil addiction. Finally, the gadfly had to believe in Inchoate's cure. Inchoate's distrustful nature made this goal almost impossible. His goal was to find this gadfly and avoid detection from the humans at the same time.

ROOT 5.4 — INCHOATE'S PROCESS

Inchoate finally settled on a surreptitious process for producing a gadfly that was radical and extreme. As he had done to Gregor, he used illusions to lure people far from their homes. He then enmeshed these people in a volatile dream world until their grasp on reality evaporated away. Once these people no longer knew who they were, he began to cull them for the ones with the iron will. For this, Inchoate utilized a shocking procedure. He transformed people into a grotesque agglomeration of animal and human parts. Then, in the form of Mandelbrot, he swallowed them. Inchoate's natural digestive process changed the agglomerated into distinct groups. Those with the least will would cave into their insect component and evolve into the form-loving ants. Those with a little stronger volition would become one of the herd animals that continuously migrated through the labyrinth. The agglomerated with wills vigorous enough to become something other than insect or herd animals were exceedingly rare. Most of these rare individuals became non-herd animals such as badgers, foxes or dogs. The rarest gems among the agglomerated were those that his bowels did not transform at all. Eventually Inchoate's bowels would reject them, and they would migrate up his body. Inchoate would feel the pressure building and would have just enough time to transform into Mandelbrot. As the huge tree, he could regurgitate the agglomerated individual without ripping apart his own body. A few moments later, the expelled individuals would awaken.

Out of the millions that Inchoate had swallowed, he had only expelled about twenty. Of these twenty, he hadn't been able to impart wisdom onto any of them. On the first expulsion, Inchoate didn't bother transforming back into his original form. Number one saw Mandelbrot and fled for fear he would be swallowed into the bowels once again. On the second expulsion, Inchoate couldn't quite regain his original form quickly enough. Number two awoke just in time to see shrinking branches withdraw into Inchoate's body. He deduced that Inchoate was Mandelbrot and fled just as the first had. For the third through tenth candidates, Inchoate made certain he was not within sight of the individuals when they awoke. Inchoate actually succeeded in talking to these candidates, but he came no closer to imparting wisdom to them. They were furious with

Mandelbrot for swallowing them and only wanted to know how they could exact revenge upon him. Inchoate tried mightily to wrest those individual's focus away from revenge, but he could not.

For numbers eleven through twenty, Inchoate added singing to his list of precautions. His immortal voice was immeasurably beautiful and mesmerized anyone who was listening. Inchoate exploited this moment of tranquility to gently remind numbers eleven through twenty about Mandelbrot. His modus operandi was to mention a tree in conversation, causing the candidates to remember Mandelbrot by themselves. Despite Inchoate's new precautions, he still could not find success. Number eleven through fifteen lost their feelings of tranquility soon after remembering Mandelbrot, and wanted to exact revenge upon him.

For numbers sixteen through twenty, he added yet another precaution. He sought to diffuse the individual's anger by blurring the target of their revenge. Inchoate tried to persuade them that Mandelbrot was not an actual being but some kind of symbolic representation of society's problems. Numbers sixteen, seventeen and eighteen didn't accept his weak and fuzzy argument. They became deeply suspicious of Inchoate and humored him until he was finished talking. Then they "escaped" from the plateau and spent the rest of their lives avoiding large trees. Numbers nineteen and twenty were Inchoate's biggest disappointments. They actually accepted Inchoate's weak argument that Mandelbrot was some kind of symbol—but only because they were dullards. Inchoate discovered soon thereafter, much to his dismay, that he could impart no wisdom to those two. Eventually, he had to cut his losses and ask the dullards to leave his plateau. Instead of returning to earth as enriching gadflies, they returned as wearisome blowhards. Both of them currently host radio shows with which to this very day they contribute greatly to Inchoate's distrust of people.

    Despite all these failures, the driven Inchoate could not give up. He had a radical new step in mind for his twenty-first ascender. He was planning on performing brain surgery on Mr. Hectic Norder.

ROOT 5.5 — HINTS OF MANDELBROT

Hectic gazed upon Inchoate for a while. "You sing beautifully," he finally said. Inchoate ignored Hectic and continued to sing. Hectic stood there dreamily for a few moments more before speaking again. "Did you invent that song yourself?" he asked. Again, Inchoate ignored him and continued to sing.

Hectic simply smiled and looked lazily around. On the periphery furthest from the vineyard, the clearing ended in a sheer cliff. Directly above the cliff, the sky turned from gold to blue and the sun shined from deep in the western horizon. Hectic stood silently entranced for so long that the sun had sunk visibly closer to the horizon by the time he finally spoke. "You must be very gifted to spontaneously create music like that," he said. Inchoate had been waiting for Hectic to say something like that and had a prepared response.

He abruptly stopped singing, whipped melodramatically around, and glared at Hectic. "Spontaneous!" he roared. "I do not create anything beautiful spontaneously. My ideas crumble inside of me like dried mud, and I struggle against despair."

Inchoate looked at Hectic to see how he was reacting. All Hectic did was smile. "Once, I used to live with the other animals of the forest," Inchoate said. "Whenever I worked on my music, they covered their ears in disgust and demanded I stop. I tried to convince them I was creating something beautiful, but they pointed at me and laughed. Their cruel treatment thrust me into a bog of misery where I was too wretched to concentrate on anything. My frustration grew too great for me to handle, and I often flew into wild rages. The animals concluded I was insane and voted to have me banished from the forest." Inchoate paused again, and again Hectic responded with a smile. "Now, I live alone on this plateau. Sometimes I can hear their snickering laughter echoing in the canyons of my mind, and I wish that I really could spontaneously create beautiful music. Sadly, I cannot. I cannot simply start my music from the beginning and precede one note at a time until the end. My ideas live inside of me for a second, and then they splinter apart like fractured bones. I must piece them together and give flesh to the frame. I can only create a little order at a time. I always feel that my efforts are futile and that I will never finish what I start. Yet, my nature compels me to create!" Inchoate finished speaking and looked studiously at Hectic.

Hectic continued to smile.

After a pause, Inchoate continued. "I must create for myself, and not for anyone else." Again, he looked at Hectic studiously; and again, Hectic just stood there smiling. Then Inchoate said, "I am glad you have come to my lonely plateau. For hundreds of years, I have longed for someone to hear me sing."

Hectic still stood there looking tranquil, but his smile had faded just a tad. A tiny part of his mind was no longer content and was thinking about what Inchoate had said. Finally Hectic spoke. "I think you just contradicted yourself. If you only create for yourself, why would you care if I heard your music?" Inchoate smiled; the process was going smoothly. Now was the time to remind Hectic of Mandelbrot.

He began stroking the trunk of the olive tree with his shadowy pawhand. "Look at Tree," he said. "The leaves, twigs, branches and roots all combine to give Tree form. There are certain resources Tree must have in order to continue existing. Tree must have water, minerals, and air. Yet, even with all those resources Tree is but an empty shell. Even with all of this, Tree's form would crumble. The leaves would fall off, the branches would break, and the bark would wither away into dust. Then, his trunk would break when the winds blew, and Tree would crumble into chaos.

"Once, Tree was no larger than a shoot of grass. Slowly, he was able to gather a little energy from the few leaves he had. His trunk grew thicker, his branches took shape, and his roots spread into the soil. Now, he is big and beautiful." Inchoate remained silent for a moment, and his organs pulsed with light. He looked expectedly at Hectic, "From where do tree leaves get their energy?" He asked.

"The sun," replied Hectic. Inchoate frowned. He was a bit frustrated with Hectic's answer. "Sun!" he bayed as flecks of yellow radiated from his torso. "Of course, you are right! Sun's rays pass through the leaves and imbue Tree with the strength to draw resources from Earth. Sun's rays give Tree form! All conscious creatures are like that olive tree. Rays of knowledge pass though us. If we want our existence to have any meaning, we must reassemble what we learn. We must create, and pass our energy to others. If we do not pass on our knowledge, we are nothing more than lifeless rocks absorbing heat." Inchoate paused and waited for Hectic to say something, but he did not. Inchoate continued.

"With my voice, I reassemble what passes through me and rise above the chaos. I tap into the trunk of our existence and feel the energy of those that have created before me. The energy of the musicians and storytellers of long ago, whose energy still flows through the trunk, inspire me to create more songs. When I finally do succeed in creating a living breathing piece of work, the joy I feel far outweighs the suffering I endured. When I sing my completed works, my energy inspires others. They in turn impart their energy to the trunk and make my existence more meaningful than ever.

"Therefore, as I sing for you, I am also singing for myself. I feel my energy passing from me to others, and I see my trunk growing thicker. To live is to create; to create is to rediscover what was already there. When I sing, I strengthen my connection with others and give meaning to existence. If we do not create, then tree crumbles. Order collapses into disorder. Sticks and branches break off and rot. Chaos is all that remains."

Inchoate ended his rush of words and looked hopefully at Hectic. Hectic simply shrugged his shoulders and smiled peacefully.

Inchoate waited a bit more and then said. "Our energy flows through the tree." An awkward moment of silence followed with Inchoate waiting and Hectic smiling. "We are all in the tree!" Inchoate bellowed.

ROOT 5.6 — HECTIC REMEMBERS MANDELBROT

Hectic's smile evaporated. "Mandelbrot!" he yelled.

"Did he swallow you?" asked Inchoate.

"Yes," said Hectic, "but how did you know that?"

"Uhmm, I have heard that he swallows folks," said Inchoate. "Why did he swallow you?"

Hectic looked perplexed. "I don't know. He said he was sick and that I was his medication, then he just swallowed me. I was just in him not too long ago. He must be close by. Do you know where he is?"

"No," replied Inchoate. I only know he is not on this plateau "The only tree here is this olive tree."

"But he must be close by," insisted Hectic, I was just in him. "You must have some idea of where he is.

Inchoate was getting worried. This was not the way his plan was supposed to unfold. Hectic was becoming skeptical far more quickly than he had anticipated. Inchoate knew that if Hectic became too skeptical, he would not receive the memories that Inchoate wanted to implant in him. Inchoate could not think of a good answer as to why he didn't know where Mandelbrot was, so he decided to shift the conversation away from that.

"Congratulations!" he blurted.

"Congratulations for what?" asked Hectic

"You have survived the metabolization." Hectic shook his grotesque head.

"What are you talking about?" he asked.

"I'm the cure," Inchoate declared.

"Mandelbrot swallowed me, not you," said Hectic. "If you were his cure, wouldn't he have swallowed you instead?"

"Fair question," said Inchoate. "To be more precise, I am the final step in his metabolization of you."

"How can we be partaking in Mandelbrot's metabolism if we are not inside him" asked Hectic."

Inchoate shook his head. "You are not physically inside him," said Inchoate, "but you are inside of him. You see Mandelbrot is not an actual physical being."

"Well," snapped Hectic, "he actually physically swallowed me."

"No he didn't" said Inchoate. "Mandelbrot is the greatest illusionist in this world. He tricked your mind into thinking he swallowed you. You were never inside of anyone. Mandelbrot is not even a tree. That is only a form he assumed to interact with you."

"Who is he then?" Hectic asked

"He is all that is living," Inchoate answered. "He is the supernatural spirit that arises from the vast and infinitely rich interconnections that all living creatures share with each other. At this time, we are all sick. The cure for this sickness is the insight I will give you. You must disperse this insight throughout the consciousness of all living beings, for the consciousness of all living beings is Mandelbrot. This is the essence of Mandelbrot's cure."

"No," said Hectic, "that was the essence of gobbledygook. You're pathetic!" Hectic turned his back from Inchoate and began to walk away.

"You're right!" shouted Inchoate "I am pathetic." Hectic stopped in his tracks, but did not turn around. "I have been alone on this plateau for hundreds of years, and I have had no one to talk to. I didn't tell you where Mandelbrot was because I didn't want you to leave so soon."

Hectic whipped around and glared at Inchoate "You didn't want me to leave!" he yelled.

"No," sobbed Inchoate as crocodile tears dripped into his muzzle. "I am so lonely." The manipulative Inchoate put on such a pitiful air, that Hectic couldn't help but feel sorry for him. The anger on Inchoate's boar face melted away as did the disgust on the other two faces.

"You could have just told me that up front," said Hectic.

"I know." Inchoate practically whimpered. "I'm sorry. I don't blame you for wanting to leave."

"Well," said Hectic, "I don't have to leave just yet. I don't see the harm in talking to you for a little while."

"Would you really do that for me?" asked Inchoate. Hectic nodded his head.

"Why not?" he asked. "Let's sit down in the shade of the olive tree and talk for a bit." Hectic didn't notice; but Inchoate abruptly stopped crying, and his tears evaporated into little puffs of smoke.

"Oh you are too kind," he said. After they had sat down under the olive tree, an awkward pause ensued where neither of them said anything. Hectic broke the silence first. "What would you like to talk about?" he asked. Inchoate shrugged his shoulders and said, "I want to talk about whatever you want to talk about."

Hectic shrugged his shoulders back.

"Okay," he said. "Where were you born?"

ROOT 5.7 — INCHOATE SPINS A YARN

rootlet 5.71 — Yellow

Inchoate began furiously spinning a yarn inside his head. He could feel the threads coming together, but he still needed a few moments more to develop a coherent story "I am not exactly sure where or when I was born," he began.

Hectic frowned. "You must know that," he said

"Time and place loses meaning where you are as old as I am." Inchoate replied.

"How old are you?" Hectic asked. Inchoate thought for a moment. "At the very least, I would say I am no less than one hundred thousand years old."

"Wow!" said Hectic. "Well then, tell me your first memory."

"My first memory is of boredom and darkness. I remember groping around in my surroundings. Eventually, I came to a spot where there was a shining light. I moved toward the light and came out from a cave and into a world. The world was rich with rocks, plants, and animals too numerous for me to list. For many years, I explored this new rich world with delight. After a few hundred years, the novelty wore off, and I became very bored.

"After a few hundred seconds, the novelty of your story is wearing off," said Hectic. "For someone who has longed to speak to someone for hundreds of years, you don't have much to stay."

"I'm sorry," said Inchoate. "I didn't expect a visit today. After so many years of solitude, I am out of practice with storytelling. Besides, you asked me about my first memories. Those were so long ago, they are tough for me to vividly remember. The only clear impression I have from my early days was that I was quite bored. Unfortunately, all the particular memories from that time of my life are an indistinguishable blur in my mind. For all I know, they could have lasted a hundred days, or hundreds of years."

"Well then," said Hectic. "Tell me your first distinct memory?" Conveniently for Inchoate, his spinning mind had just connected enough threads to tell a story. And so he began…

"I clearly remember something that happened after my first bout of boredom," he said. On that morning, I awoke to a particularly feverish attack of boredom."

"You sure are bored quite a bit," said Hectic. "What did you do?"

"I was feeling restless, so I began rubbing two sticks together," said Inchoate. "Soon, I noticed that the sticks were getting warm. The harder I rubbed the sticks together, the more heat they produced. Eventually, a bright speck flew from the sticks and landed on one of the leaves. The speck began to glow a little brighter and bigger. Suddenly the speck transformed into a little dancing yellow. Yellow loved to eat, so I began to feed him,"

"What did yellow eat?" asked Hectic.

"He especially liked dried leaves and sticks," said Inchoate. "The more I fed him, the bigger he became. Eventually, I tired of watching Yellow dance; so I stomped on him and he went away."

"Did you ever bring Yellow back?" asked Hectic.

"Compulsively," said Inchoate. "I became addicted to creating him. In the days that followed, I recreated Yellow thousands of times to alleviate my boredom. "That's all you did?" Hectic asked. "You just created and destroyed him?"

"No," said Inchoate. "At some point I began dancing with Yellow. Sometimes, Yellow and I would dance all night."

Hectic gave Inchoate a bemused look. "For how many days did you dance with Yellow?

"I'm not sure," said Inchoate. "All those days I danced with yellow are an indistinguishable blur in my mind. The one day that I remember the most vividly was the very last day I danced with him." Inchoate stopped talking, stood up and turned away from Hectic.

"Well don't stop now," said Hectic. "I'm just getting interested. What happened?" Inchoate turned back around and faced Hectic. Except for a few flickers of yellow, his torso had grown dark. He began to vibrate imperceptibly. The soothing sounds of a crackling fire began to emanate from his stomach, and the little flickers of yellow on his torso coalesced into an image of a fire.

Inchoate began to speak again. His voice had become low and seemed to emanate from everywhere. "There had been a drought," he said, "and most the vegetation had browned and wilted. On that day, Yellow grew at a rate much faster than I was accustomed to." The playful little flames upon Inchoate began to dance exactly like a real fire. Suddenly, the flames on Inchoate's torso doubled in size and roared.

Hectic was fixated upon the fiery display on Inchoate's torso. "What did you do?"

"I became alarmed and started to stomp on him," answered Inchoate. Upon Inchoate's stomach, Hectic saw the black image of a foot stomp down upon the fire. "Unlike the previous times," said Inchoate, "yellow refused to die and simply danced around my foot. I panicked and gave Yellow a swift kick." There was a loud snap and Inchoate's stomach seemed to explode sparks straight towards Hectic. Hectic winced and closed his eyes. When he opened them again, he found himself sitting on a parched landscape. All around him, hundreds of Yellows flickered into creation and began to dance. As they danced, they grew quickly and merged together. In the landscape, Hectic saw Inchoate. Inchoate turned to run, but Yellow roared out to him.

"Stop Inchoate or I will stomp you out!" Inchoate stopped and turned back towards Yellow. Yellow had flared all the way to the sky and was eating the trees. He had developed a rudimentary face, which included two black voids for eyes. Yellow focused his voids downward and looked disdainfully upon Inchoate. "Tell me Inchoate!" he roared. "Tell me why I should not stomp you out as you have stomped me out a thousand times." As he spoke, a third black void opened and closed below his eyes.

"If I had known you were living, I would not have stomped you out," Inchoate shouted back. Yellow reared his head and howled. A thick mane of flames issued forth from his head and turned the sky orange.

"My life force is beyond question," replied Yellow. "Since I am me, I can directly experience my emotions and thoughts. You, on the other hand, are not me. I'm not completely sure that you are truly alive." Yellow lifted a great flaming foot, which he poised menacingly over Inchoate's head. Inchoate quickly tried to reason with him.

"Yellow, you at least acknowledge there is a possibility that I am alive, don't you?"

"Yes, there is that possibility," said Yellow.

"Then why not err on the side of safety and spare me?" Inchoate asked.

"I know you're alive," crackled Yellow. "I'm just playing with you, because I'm bored. I like playing with you Inchoate. Having complete control over your life makes me feel important."

Yellow stopped talking and stared maliciously upon Inchoate. Then, he began to speak in the cruelly feigned voice of a detached intellect.

"For the world's sake, I have to be careful with you. If I let you procreate, you will multiply and become more difficult to squelch. You will quickly burn through all the resources that exist before finally resorting to cannibalism. Therefore, your continued existence threatens the life of every other creature. Your one life cannot possibly outweigh the innumerable lives that populate this world. I'm sorry, Inchoate. I have no choice but to stamp you out. Take heart," Yellow said with a smirk. "I will probably recreate you another day when the whim strikes me."

As Yellow stomped his gargantuan flaming foot down on Inchoate, Hectic looked away from the horrific scene. Then, he heard Yellow scream. Hectic turned his head back and saw that Yellow had devoured everything in the land. With nothing left to sustain him, Yellow rapidly shrank until he barely reached Inchoate's knee.

Inchoate looked down upon Yellow exactly as Yellow had looked down upon him. The gaping black holes that were once his eyes had become expressionless pinpricks. Inchoate could have ended him with a stomp, but he seemed to be enjoying watching Yellow struggle to exist. Yellow flickered feebly for a little while, and then died out with a wheeze. Hectic's vision was blurring, and he was becoming very dizzy.

He closed his eyes and took a few deep breaths.

"Are you still listening to me?" asked Inchoate. Hectic opened his eyes. The images from Inchoate's story were gone, and Hectic was still sitting beneath the olive tree with Inchoate.

"Did you fall asleep on me?" said Inchoate.

"No," said Hectic. "I just closed my eyes for a second, because I felt dizzy. I heard everything you said. Please continue your story. I'm very interested."

"From the spot where Yellow died," said Inchoate "a thread of smoke wafted upwards and frayed away into nothingness. All around me, the landscape was a blackened, smoldering wasteland of utter boredom. I decided to leave the wasteland of boredom and go somewhere more interesting."

"Where did you go?" asked Hectic.

"I began walking towards the western horizon," Inchoate replied.

rootlet 5.72 — the valley animals

"I had not realized how big Yellow had been or the extent of the damage he had wrought. The world, I learned, was much larger than I had imagined. I walked for many years through the blackened land of boredom before finally coming to the edge of a great ocean. I waded into the water and began swimming out to sea. After swimming for several years, I came to the shores of a land that Yellow had not destroyed. I emerged from the ocean and climbed up a mountain beyond the rocky shore. On the other side of the mountain was a valley. As I looked down into the valley, I saw thousands of creatures. Until then, I had not known that any other creatures existed in the world except for me."

"You must have been excited," said Hectic.

"I was," replied Inchoate, "but I was also quite apprehensive. I had no idea how these other creatures would react toward me, nor did I know how to react towards them. I decided to stay on the mountaintop and observe them from afar." Inchoate fell silent and rested his jaw upon his handpaw in a contemplative posture.

"What did you observe?" asked Hectic after a long pause.

"The creatures lived in families of two to twenty. Most of these families resided in the most basic shelter."

"What do you mean by basic?" asked Hectic.

"Anything that would protect them from the elements," replied Inchoate, "A crevice between some boulders, a tree hollow, or a hole in the ground. A few of them did live in huts, but these were only primitive constructions of stone, dirt and wood."

"Sounds like they had some kind of community," said Hectic. "Did you see them interact with each other?"

"Yes," said Inchoate. "Belying their rudimentary domiciles was a sophisticated community whose individual members had sundry specialties. The adult creatures spent their days creating products or performing services that other animals within their community could utilize. They then bartered their goods and services amongst each other."

"That is amazing," said Hectic. "What in particular did they trade?" Inchoate paused.

"Oh I can't remember all the details," he said. "I do remember watching rabbits harvest some carrots, which they traded to some bears. In return, the bears built a stone walkway to the entrance of the rabbit's home."

"What else did they do?" Hectic asked. Inchoate thought for a moment.

"They harvested crops, built homes and vast assortments of items; they created everything from barrels to baked goods. Do you know what I really remember about them?" Inchoate asked.

"What?" asked Hectic?

"As I was watching them," said Inchoate, "I remember longing to be part of a community. That was a new sensation for me."

"Aside from Yellow, you never had company," said Hectic. "I'm not surprised that upon seeing fellow creatures you developed that longing."

"I wanted more than company," replied Inchoate. "I wanted a sense of purpose and fellow creatures with whom I could interact. I wanted to have a place in the world where others needed me."

"I assume eventually you mustered up the courage to enter the valley and introduce yourself?"

"Yes, eventually I entered the valley," said Inchoate. Inchoate stopped talking and looked away from Hectic. After a few moments Hectic got impatient.

"Did you introduce yourself or not?" he asked.

"I did not need to introduce myself," said Inchoate. "They somehow already know who I was, and they hated me." Much to Hectic's shock, Inchoate grotesquely flexed his jaw into an impossible grimace. The middle of his mouth crimped; the corners opened wide. His mouth looked like an hourglass tipped over to a side. Inchoate began to talk out of the left portion of his mouth without moving the right portion. "Go away Inchoate," said left side mouth. "We don't want you here to ruin our village." The left of Inchoate's face took on a baleful appearance while the right side remained emotionless. Inchoate modified his vibrations and created an effect that sounded like multitudes of creatures speaking in chorus. In this chorus voice, he repeated what he had just said out of left mouth again. "Go away Inchoate, we don't want you here to ruin our village."

The right of Inchoate's face adopted a devastated expression and drooped. Tears trickled from his right eyes and stained his fur.

The breathing out of his right mouth became halting and staccato. Inchoate shifted his right eye leftward, so his right side could address his left side. The sight of the baleful eye on the left side upset his right side so much that right eye had to look away from left eye. Righty looked at the ground and spoke to Lefty as best he could.

"I cannot bear to be alone anymore," said Righty. "All I want is to join your village and become friends with all of you." Poor Righty—the more he pleaded with Lefty the more hatred gushed from Lefty's side. Inchoate adjusted his vibrations, and the chorus broke into an angry rabble of barks, growls, hisses squeaks, and squawks. Inchoate picked up a rock with his left handpaw, and smacked the right side of his face. Righty screamed, but the rabble from lefty only intensified. Inchoate began to ferociously beat the right side of his face with all the intensity hatred could muster

"Stop!" said Hectic. "You're hurting yourself." Inchoate uncrimped his mouth and his face returned to normal.

"I have no bones, and my flesh is very pliable," he said. "I cannot hurt myself. Besides, I thought a little performance art would greatly enhance the story."

"Actually," said Hectic, "I find the face contortion and self-flagellation very distracting." I'd feel more comfortable if you told the story with only words."

Inchoate shrugged his shoulders. "Suit yourself," he said. "Now, Where was I?" he asked.

"See, you even distracted yourself." said Hectic. "You were just describing to me how the animals violently rejected you."

"Oh yeah," said Inchoate. "Anyways, I scrambled all the way back up the mountain. At the top, I collapsed in exhaustion. There I lay unable to move for a month."

"But you said you couldn't be hurt," said Hectic.

"Oh, I wasn't physically hurt," said Inchoate. "I just didn't move for a month."

"Why not?" Hectic asked.

"Well," said Inchoate "because sorrow made my flesh a thousand times heavier than normal."

Hectic snorted. "So you're saying the animals hurt your feelings very badly,"

"Yes," Inchoate said. "They really did hurt my feelings quite badly,"

"Oh brother," said Hectic. "Did you finally lighten up after a month?"

"Yes," Inchoate replied. "My flesh became lighter and I spent days just pacing back and forth on the mountain."

"Why were you pacing so much?" Hectic asked.

"I was devising a scheme to integrate myself into the village."

Hectic chuckled. "I don't think you had much of a chance to integrate yourself with such a hostile hurtful crowd."

Inchoate smiled. "Wait till you hear my plan," he gushed. "I decided to disguise myself as one of the baby rabbits."

Hectic shrugged his shoulders.

"Why a baby rabbit?"

"When I was observing the animals," said Inchoate, "I noticed that the rabbit family had the most offspring. I figured that mother rabbit might not notice the addition of one more,"

Hectic shot Inchoate a skeptical look. "How did that work out for you?" he asked

"When night fell, I kneaded my body into the form of a rabbit. I furtively hopped down the mountain to a space between the roots of an old tree stump where the rabbit's denned. I snuck into the hole and crept down a gently sloping tunnel. At the end of the tunnel, the family of rabbits was sleeping together in their cozy den. All the little ones were snuggled up against their mother. I carefully wedged myself between two kits and went to sleep," said Inchoate

"They didn't reject you?" Hectic asked.

"Not exactly," replied Inchoate.

"What does 'not exactly' mean?" asked Hectic.

"Well, the next morning when everyone woke up, I was overjoyed that my presence did not seem to disturb any of the rabbits," said Inchoate. "Nobody pushed me away or asked me to leave."

"So they accepted you." said Hectic.

Inchoate sighed. "Not really," he said. "Over the next few days I learned that just because they didn't overtly reject me, did not mean that they accepted me."

"Explain what you mean," demanded Hectic.

"The mother licked and groomed each of her cubs, but she did not do the same for me. The kits played rambunctiously with each other, but they did not play with me." Inchoate paused and thought for a moment. "They moved around me," he said finally, "as if I was an inanimate object—a stone or piece of wood that happened to be in their den."

"How did the other animals react to you when you ventured out from the rabbit's den?" Hectic asked.

"They were as unresponsive to my presence as the rabbits had been," Inchoate said. "When I spoke to them, they seemed to not hear me. At first, I thought that their sensory organs were not capable of perceiving my presence. However, I noticed that if they happened to be walking toward me, they would always change direction to avoid hitting me."

"Perhaps they were making a concerted effort to ignore you," Hectic said. Inchoate nodded his head. "I considered that," he replied. "I did an experiment where I would sneak up on one of the animals and make a loud noise to startle them. If they reacted, I figured that would prove they were deliberately trying to ignore me.

"So what happened," Hectic asked.

"What happened was complicated," said Inchoate. "When the sound originated directly from me - such as when I yelled or clapped - they did not react. However, if the sound came indirectly from me - such as when I hit the ground with a stick - they would react. Yet, as soon as they turned and saw me, their minds appeared to delete my presence from their consciousnesses. They always immediately returned to what they were doing as if nothing had happened."

"That is puzzling," said Hectic,"

"I believe I was a void in their awareness. On a purely non-conscious level, they seemed to sense my mass taking up space."

"So, their rudimentary perception of you was enough for them to maneuver around you—but nothing more," said Hectic.

"Exactly," said Inchoate.

"So how did this play out?" Hectic asked. Inchoate hesitated. His mind was running out of yarn.

rootlet 5.73 — the learning place

"Honestly," he said, "I can't remember much about the following few hundred years. I know I changed families several times, as animals tend to age quickly and die. At some point, I reverted back to my true form."

Hectic thought for several seconds before speaking. "Did you stay in the valley in your true form?" he asked.

"Yes, I was there for quite some time in my true form," said Inchoate.

"How come the animals didn't kick you out?" asked Hectic.

"Why would they?" asked Inchoate.

"Because they could see you," said Hectic. "You were in your original from." Inchoate froze. He realized he had talked himself into an inconsistency, and his imagination was failing him. The image of a school randomly popped into his head. Not knowing what else to do, he went with that.

"Oh, wait," he said. "Now I remember what happened. The animals could see me after they finished construction of the learning place?"

"The what," said Hectic.

"The Learning Place," replied Inchoate.

"After they built this learning place, they could suddenly see you?" asked Hectic.

"Yes," said Inchoate.

"Why," Hectic asked.

"I'm not sure," said Inchoate, "but that's what happened."

"Did you stay in the valley?" Hectic asked.

"Inchoate shrugged his shoulders. "Yeah," he said. "Why wouldn't I."

"I don't understand," said Hectic. "Why did they accept you? Why didn't they drive you from their valley like before?"

"Oh," said Inchoate abruptly. "They didn't just accept me. They told me if I wanted to stay in the valley, I would have to attend the LP five days a week."

"You mean the Learning Place?" Hectic asked.

"Yes, that," said Inchoate.

"What exactly was that?" asked Hectic

"The LP was the building they were constructing which would soon house their programs to annihilate chaos."

"Why did they want to annihilate chaos?" Hectic asked.

"Their actual target was suffering" said Inchoate. "They believed that chaos was the mother of suffering. They wanted to kill the mother, so that she could never give birth."

"What were they talking about?" said Hectic. "Chaos is capable of anything and is, therefore, the mother of everything."

"And I agree," said Inchoate, "but the PAS saw things differently,"

"The what?" asked Hectic.

"The PAS – Parents Against Suffering," said Inchoate.

"I don't understand this…this PAS," said Hectic. "What were they thinking?"

"The PAS believed that no one would logically choose suffering. Therefore, they thought suffering could only result from the unpredictable situations that stem from chaos," said Inchoate.

"Let me see if I have this straight," Hectic said. "The PAS believed that they were going to institute some programs that would rid the entire world of chaos. That seems absurd!"

"I agree," said Inchoate. "But you must understand that the whole world to the PAS was only their valley. They did not know anything else."

"I can't believe that," said Hectic. "Some of them must have ventured beyond the valley at some point."

Inchoate shook his head. "No," he said, "None of them ever did.

"None of them...ever?" asked Hectic.

"No," Inchoate replied. "Their minds were incapable of even imagining a world beyond the valley."

"Even if that were true," said Hectic, "some of them would have surely wandered out of the valley by pure chance."

"That could not have happened," said Inchoate,

"Why not?" asked Hectic.

"Their brains were constituted in such a way that they were unaware of the actual boundary. If one of them happened to come to the edge of the valley, they would simply change their direction without any awareness of what they were doing," said Inchoate.

"Wow," said Hectic. "So you're saying the boundary that restricted them was incomprehensible to them as well"

"Exactly," answered Inchoate

"Did you attempt to simply tell them of the world beyond?" Hectic asked.

"I did," said Inchoate. "I told them several times during the period they could see me."

"What did they say?" Hectic asked.

"Gesundheit," replied Inchoate,

"Gesundheit? Why would they say that?" Hectic asked

"They were incapable of hearing words that expressed the idea of a world beyond the valley. I must have sounded to them like I was just making noise. I suspect they thought I was sneezing."

Hectic shook his hybrid head. "Even if they could not imagine a world beyond, they must have noticed the chaos within their valley. Did you try and show them the infinite shapes of clouds, or the tangle of roots fighting for soil in a rocky forest floor?" Hectic asked.

"I showed them things like that;" said Inchoate, "but their minds could not see chaos. In the clouds, they always saw symmetrical geometric shapes like cubes and pyramids. On the forest floor, where you or I would see an incomprehensible jumble of tree roots, they saw an ordered lattice. Their minds projected order on everything. Anything that was irregular or chaotic did not register on their conscious," said Inchoate.

They obviously saw chaos somewhere," said Hectic, "that was what they were so bent on annihilating." Inchoate smiled wryly.

"The animals could see chaos in only one place—themselves," said Inchoate. "For them, nature was a static assortment of simple objects and forces for them to act upon. They could not conceive of themselves as being a part of nature, nor could they conceive of nature acting upon them. That quirky mental limitation of theirs meant that they conceived of themselves as the only source of chaos and order in the world."

A flash of enlightenment flicked into Hectic's six eyes. "I bet they were designing the LP to be a training center for rational thought," he said. "They must have thought that if they made themselves rational, then the entire world would be rational."

"You are right," said Inchoate. They became obsessed with order and rational thought. They thought if they were rational, then the world would be rational. If the world was rational, then the world would be predictable. If the world was predictable, then everyone could avoid suffering. If everyone could avoid suffering, then everyone would be happy. Therefore, in their minds, rational thought would make the world a happy place."

"Now I'm intrigued," said Hectic. Did they ever get the LP up and running?"

"Oh yes," said Inchoate. "The PAS assembled the finest stonemasons and carpenters in the valley." When they finished making the structure, the PAS hired some animals that were knowledgeable enough to teach the necessary skills."

"You had to go to this learning place—right?" said Hectic. Inchoate looked confused for a second.

"Of course," he said suddenly. "Of course I did."

"What was that like?" Hectic asked. Inchoate shifted nervously.

"Well," said Inchoate." On the day the learning place opened, parents all through the valley lovingly jostled their offspring out of bed and forced them to quickly eat their breakfasts. Then, they shuffled them off to the Learning Place."

"I figured that!" Hectic huffed. "I want to know what went on inside the learning place." Inchoate fell silent, as his mind drew a blank.

"At the learning place, the educators gave the young one's mental exercises designed to develop basic skills." Hectic narrowed his eyes and focused in on Inchoate.

"Why are you so vague?"

"Listen," said Inchoate. "This was a long time ago, and I was only there for a few days."

"You just told me that you attended the learning place for several years."

"I did," said Inchoate, "but that was many decades after the initial opening. When they initially opened the LP, the PAS had many problems and had to close the place down."

"Oh, now I understand what you're saying," said Hectic. "So, what were the problems?"

"The LP bored almost all of the youngsters to tears," answered Inchoate. "They simply could not sit and focus on their studies. Over the course of a week, they began to rock increasingly more vigorously in their chairs. At the end of that initial week, the youngsters looked like they were in the throes of a mass epileptic fit. Many of them were writhing so much, they broke their chairs."

Hectic laughed. "What did the PAS think about that?" he asked.

"The PAS hired some experts on youngster development," said Inchoate. "They initiated a massive study on the problem of distractibility. After many years, they finally concluded that the walls were not homogeneous enough."

"Not homogeneous enough?" said Hectic, bemused.

"Yes," said Inchoate. The experts said the nooks, crannies and tiny protuberances, which are typical of stone walls, were distracting the youngsters from their studies."

"Did the PAS homogenize the walls?" Hectic asked.

"Yes," said Inchoate. "They meticulously worked over every spot of the LP until those walls were smooth as glass."

Hectic shook his head. "I'm sure the new smooth walls did not improve the youngsters' behavior," he said.

"No, they did not," confirmed Inchoate.

"What did the idiot PAS do then?" Hectic asked.

"They painted the walls a homogenous white," replied Inchoate.

"I thought they already homogenized the walls," said Hectic.

"They homogenized the wall's texture but not their color," Inchoate clarified. "You see the experts—"

Hectic was getting impatient. "I get the picture," he said testily. "Listen, we have talked for a long while, and I am growing weary. "Can we wrap this up?"

"My apologies," said Inchoate. "I did not intend to talk for such a long time. I just have had no one –"

"I know, I know" said Hectic as he waved his arms in the air. "You've been alone for such a long time. Why don't you just skip to the last step in the chronology of the Learning place."

Inchoate continued. "Ultimately, the LP was a huge failure." He said. "The youngsters hated the training program so much, that they would flee from the LP whenever the opportunity came to them."

"I assume the PAS gave up at this point," said Hectic.

"No," said Inchoate." The PAS decided to dig a trench around the LP to contain the kids,"

"I don't believe you," said Hectic. "The PAS would have realized that many animals could simply climb in and out of a trench."

"They did realize that," said Inchoate. That's why they were planning to fill the trench with water and flesh-eating fish."

"Hectic rolled his six eyes. "You making this up," he said. "No one built a moat with killer fish."

"I never said they built the moat, I only said they planned to," said Inchoate.

"Whatever," said Hectic.

"No, listen," said Inchoate. "When they dug about twenty feet down, a viscous, black fluid exploded from the trench floor."

Hectic jumped to his hooves. "Are you talking about crude?" he asked.

"That's what I'm talking about," replied Inchoate. "Like the cells within Mandelbrot's body, the animals soon learned to utilize the awesome energy of crude. With this energy, they were able to solve their problems of the youngsters escaping. Indeed, after a time the youngsters ceased trying to escape. They even were able to perpetually focus on their LP exercises." Inchoate sensed that Hectic would not wonder how he knew about Mandelbrot's cells, and he was right.

"How did the crude help them to do that?" Hectic asked.

"The animals used the energy from crude to engage in an endless project of perpetually adding additions to the LP. In a few generations, the LP's size exponentially increased and engulfed the entire valley. In the end, the animals unwittingly encased themselves within the LP."

"Didn't some of them try and escape?" Hectic asked.

"Initially, many of them did try to escape," said Inchoate, "but none of them ever did."

"I don't understand," said Hectic. "Didn't the LP have exits?"

"There were exits," said Inchoate, "but the LP had become a labyrinth of such mind-boggling proportions that no one could find them."

A look of apprehension crept into Hectic's face.

"Did this mammoth structure have a department of special problems... and a department of extra special problems?" he asked.

Inchoate ignored his question "Over time," he said. "The animals on the PAS transformed into ants and took over the bureaucratic functions of the LP. The rest of the animals performed the innumerable tasks that were necessary to keep the LP running. Soon all of them forgot about the world outside the LP. To them, the world was the LP and nothing more."

Hectic's eyes quivered as he backed away from Inchoate. Inchoate looked at him and began to roar with laughter. "Who is the pathetic one now?" He asked. "You are the one who believed the ridiculous story I invented only to amuse myself. I win!" Hectic began to stammer.

"Excuse me," he said finally.

"I win!" repeated Inchoate

"That entire story was all one massive lie?" Hectic asked.

"Uh-huh," said Inchoate.

ROOT 5.8 -- INCHOATE PERFORMS BRAIN SURGERY ON HECTIC

Inchoate began to move his eyes in the most mysterious manner. His right eye rolled rightward at a rather rapid rate, while his left eye looped leftward at a somewhat slower pace. The wild eyes entranced Hectic. He became so fixated on their irregular motion, he did not even blink. Inchoate approached Hectic until he was facing him from only a foot away. He then began to grotesquely flex his jaw into that impossible grimace. The middle of his mouth crimped; yet, the corners were open wide. His mouth again looked like an hourglass tipped over to a side. From his mouth's corners came smoke in snuffs and puffs that unfurled into the air like wispy mustache tufts. Hectic inhaled the smoke and immediately lost consciousness. As he began to fall over, Inchoate caught him and gently laid him on the ground. Inchoate stopped rolling his eyes, and the smoke ceased to effuse from him. He released his crimped grimace, and his long wolf snout grew back into place. Inchoate lowered his large black nose towards Hectic and began to sniff the entirety of his hybrid head with great intensity.

Soon, he focused his sniffing on the cranium of Hectic's middle head. After focusing in on one particular spot, Inchoate lifted his head and flexed his paws. From each digit, a claw protruded except for one. On that digit, a glistening metallic scalpel thrust out. Inchoate gently lowered the scalpel's blade to the cranium of the middle head and began to cut. He skillfully cut three sides of a rectangle into Hectic's head, but left the forth side towards the back of the cranium uncut. Then, he pried open Hectic's middle cranium from the front. The boney plate fell open like a basement trap door. Within the snaily segments of gray matter was a fist-sized mass of calcium. With unimaginable dexterity, Inchoate carefully removed the segment with his teeth and began to gingerly chew on the mass. The white shell cracked, and Inchoate carefully spit out the shards. Within his jaw, Inchoate held the former contents of the white mass—a small chunk of Hectic's brain.

Inchoate took a step back and cut open his own skull just as he had Hectic's. After flipping his cranium open, he cut loose one of his own brain segments. He then took Hectic by the shoulders and sat him up. As Inchoate held Hectic, he bowed forward and the loosened chunk tumbled from his head into Hectic's. Within the concavity left behind in Inchoate's brain, another identical chunk grew quickly into place. Inchoate lowered his jaw and dropped the segment he was holding in his mouth into Hectic's skull. The two dislodged segments were resting upon each other inside Hectic's skull. Inchoate blew smoke into Hectic's opened skull. As the smoke drifted around the segments, they fused with each other and melded into the rest of Hectic's brain. Next, Inchoate closed the bony flap on Hectic's skull and blew an opaque plume of smoke around Hectic's head. When the plume cleared, the surgical cut was completely healed.

Inchoate stepped away from Hectic and barked sharply. Hectic woke up with a start and jumped to his feet. "Stop feeling sorry for yourself," Inchoate said. Hectic looked perplexedly at Inchoate as a wave of confusion smothered his mind. The memories that Inchoate had recounted were now infused in Hectic's brain, but they did not square with Hectic's most recent memories of Inchoate recounting the story. Hectic's brain twitched a little in his head, and then his memory of Inchoate tweaked a bit to match his original memories. At that moment, Hectic believed that he was the one who had invented the story of fire and the valley animals. He believed he was the one who had just laughed in Inchoate's face and declared "I win". Hectic put his hand to his middle forehead and looked down at the ground in shame.

"I'm so sorry," he said. "I don't know why I did what I just did."

"That's okay," said Inchoate. "Your time in the bowels has damaged your mind."

Hectic was breathing heavily and his eyes flickered about. "You must be right," he said. "Why else would I tell so many lies? I must be deranged."

Inchoate smiled. "Yes," he said. "You are deranged, but I can see you have a good heart deep down underneath the chaos. If you listen to me, I can make you whole again." Hectic looked up.

"Would you do that for me?" he asked earnestly.

"Of course," said Inchoate, "but you must listen to me." Inchoate sat back down under the olive tree.

"Please," he said. "Make me whole."

"What you first must realize," said Inchoate, "is that everything is chaos."

"But if everything is chaos," said Hectic, "how can you make me whole?

"You must understand," Inchoate replied," consciousness is nothing more than the result of disruptions and disappointment."

"You are talking past me," said Hectic. "I don't understand"

"This perception of yours that I am talking past you is only a symptom of your deranged mind. You must fight this perception. Try and concentrate on what I have said about consciousness." Hectic thought for a while and then said "If consciousness is disappointment, then consciousness is misery," Inchoate shrugged his shoulders. "Maybe," he said. Hectic was shaking.

"Maybe!" screamed Hectic. "Is that all you have to offer me? You're making me feel even more deranged."

Inchoate shrugged his shoulders again. "Maybe you need to bate your disappointment long enough for you to think," he said. "Don't talk for a while, just think." Hectic took a deep breath and tried to "just think," but only the suffocating feeling of deep disappointment registered in his mind. The best Hectic could do was to think about his disappointment. Soon his thoughts evolved into cogitations on disappointment in general. In particular, he began to think about what Inchoate had said about consciousness resulting from disruption and disappointment. *Perhaps Inchoate had meant something different than what he had thought.* Suddenly, Hectic hit upon an idea that gave him hope. *Consciousness,* he thought, *could result from disappointment, but not be disappointment.* He was thinking about that, and he realized that he no longer felt frustrated or disappointed. Instead, he felt a glorious sense of wonder that compensated him one thousand times for the momentary frustration he had felt. Hectic smiled so broadly that the human portion around his chin seemed to expand a little into his grotesque head.

OFFSHOOT SIX

THE WAY BACK TO GREGOR

ROOT 6.1 — FRUSTRATION, ENERGY AND GREGOR

rootlet 6.11 — the genealogy of frustration

Hectic wanted to speak, but his desire to communicate did not stem from his usual sources of fear, anger, or selfish desire. Hectic's need stemmed from a new altruistic desire to share the contents of his mind. He looked warmly upon Inchoate and said, "Frustration is the father of wonder."

Inchoate was pleased with this development. Now that Hectic knew how to turn frustration into wonder, the earth had a chance. He said to Hectic, "Wonder is the father of opportunity."

Hectic thought hard and long about that before saying, "Frustration and will are the parents of wonder and the grandparents of opportunity."

rootlet — 6.12 creative energy and the way back to Gregor

Inchoate smiled. "You are doing well Gregor."

Hectic's smile faded. The name Gregor resonated in his mind and his brain tweaked. He suddenly remembered his former life, but those memories didn't fit with his current ones. Gregor's neurons snapped apart and reattached differently than they had been before. Gregor no longer remembered the bowels or the phony memories implanted from Inchoate. He remembered leaving Kappy's office, meeting Mandelbrot, and Mandelbrot swallowing him. Suddenly, he realized that he had not always been a grotesque monster.

"Oh my God!" screamed Gregor, "What's happened to me?"

"Touch your head," said Inchoate. Gregor touched his head and felt the smooth skin and hair of his old human head. Then he looked down upon the rest of his body, which was still a grotesque amalgamation of creatures. "What about the rest of me?" asked Gregor.

"You will fully regain your human form before the sun sets." said Inchoate. Gregor believed Inchoate simply because not believing him was too unpleasant to think about. "Don't worry," said

Inchoate. "The cure for all of us is taking hold; the initial stage has begun."

"Which is?" asked Gregor.

"The correct attitude in just one individual," replied Inchoate. "Your wonder addiction will cure society's oil addiction. From this day forth, your addiction will force you to seek out individuals with whom you sharply disagree. Since you will appreciate these oppositional voices, you will be confronting them as brothers instead of enemies. As you gain people's respect, they will acquire your contagious addiction to wonder. With so much frustration fathering so much wonder, there will be so much more opportunity for Mandelbrot to improve."

"You're talking about creative energy!" You want to plug into the world's creative energy reserves."

"Exactly," said Inchoate. "Let the creative energy flow from person to person without the tax of anger and fear. Any system we build with our hands, we must first build with our minds."

"I understand completely," said Gregor triumphantly.

"Good," said Inchoate. "Now is the time for me to initiate the second stage and plant some seeds inside your wondering mind for you to disseminate."

Gregor frowned "What if these ideas are wrong and exasperate my countries sickness?" he asked.

"They may very well be wrong," replied Inchoate. That is what stage one guards against. Your new nature will compel you to present these ideas to people with opposing views. Those people will cleanse your view of any illogic, false assumptions, or sophistry."

"Oh," said Gregor. "So these seed ideas may possibly grow into something totally different than from what they began."

"I wouldn't say possibly," replied Inchoate, "I'd say probably."

"I don't know," said Gregor. "You may be overly optimistic, but I'm very curious about your seed ideas." There was a pause and then Gregor asked, "What are your seed ideas?"

rootlet — 6.13 economic energy

Inchoate laughed. "Let the planting begins," he said. "Turn your mind to the great brain of economic creativity."

"To whom are you referring," Gregor asked, "Adam Smith, David Ricardo, John Maynard Keynes?"

"I refer to no individual person," answered Inchoate. "I am referring to the abstract creative brain." Gregor thought hard about what Inchoate meant by that. He imagined the rough and tumble nature of creativity. He imagined the brain tolerating clashing thoughts long enough for them to smash together and synthesize new thoughts. Then, he thought about the jungle of economic survival. "What if economic activities were like thoughts?" Gregor said. "A creative economic brain would allow multitudes of varied economic activities to simultaneously exist. Perhaps what you are referring to is capitalism."

"Very good," said Inchoate.

Gregor smiled. "Interesting metaphor," he said.

"Does that mean you like capitalism?" asked Inchoate.

"I like creativity, so I like capitalism." answered Gregor

"Then you must think capitalism is good, don't you?" asked Inchoate

"Naturally," replied Gregor

"Well, then you must of course believe that government should not interfere with capitalism at all," stated Inchoate. Gregor was about to say yes, but then some clashing thoughts came into his mind.

"There must be some interference," said Gregor. "Otherwise, corporations would simply dump their toxic waste into rivers. There would be no minimum wage, or board of health. There would be no one to check the sanitation of meat-processing plants or restaurants."

"Are you saying capitalism is bad?" asked Inchoate.

"Unchecked capitalism is obviously bad," replied Gregor, "but regulated capitalism, at least I think, is good." Gregor was beginning to feel a little uneasy. He was thinking more about how he had lived his life before Mandelbrot had swallowed him, and he felt a sense of shame. He really didn't know much about government and capitalism. He didn't know how he could understand how those two things interacted, when he didn't really understand those two things. Part of him didn't want to think, but the new wondering part of him wouldn't let that happen. Gregor fell silent for a long time.

Eventually, Inchoate asked him, "What are you thinking about."

"I'm thinking about people"

"Why people?" asked Inchoate

"Because people form governments and economies." Gregor replied. "If I understand their nature, then I might be able to better understand how capitalism and government intertwine."

"People are all different," said Inchoate.

"True," replied Gregor, "but the vast majority of people do share basic behavior patterns."

"Which are?" Inchoate asked.

"Well, humans have an inherent urge to control resources, so they may enjoy a high standard of living," said Gregor. "Once they obtain resources, they seek to secure them from loss. Hence, humans prefer stable environments in which they are able to protect the resources they have."

"That's hardly profound," said Inchoate.

"Simple premises are the best stepping stones to profound conclusions," said Gregor. "Please just let me finish."

"Sorry," said Inchoate with a smile. "After all of these years, I'm a little desperate for good conversation. Please continue."

"Once humans have fulfilled their primary goal of securing their resources, they move to their secondary objective—securing more resources." Inchoate looked very amused, but he said nothing. "Due to the variegation of life, some humans are able to acquire more resources than others," Gregor finished.

"Variegations?" said Inchoate. Do you mean like one person having more intelligence or drive than another?"

"That's not what I was thinking, but that is a small part—very small," replied Gregor. "Some people are able to overcome challenging boundaries with the force of their will. Unfortunately, most examples of this are restricted to people rising from the lower middle class to the upper class. What percentages of truly impoverished people are able to acquire resources? Of all those people starving in third world countries, who among them will become doctors, teachers, writers, or businessmen? How often do the impoverished ever do anything other than remain impoverished?" Gregor asked.

"Genius always finds a way," offered Inchoate.

"I don't know," Gregor sighed. "How do we measure the geniuses that didn't find a way? If Albert Einstein had been born into the impoverished masses of India would people ever have known who he was? Would we have a theory of relativity? How can we conceive of all the geniuses who perished or could not develop? How many writers, philosophers, artists and statesman have we lost?"

"When the genius sings for others is he singing for himself?" asked a grinning Inchoate.

"When any one sings for others they are singing for themselves," replied Hectic. "Creative energy longs for the liberation of all minds."

"Even the liberation of dull minds?" asked Inchoate.

"Especially the dull minds," responded Gregor. "Liberation is often what makes the dull mind brilliant. Creative energy makes everyone free. Without creativity, people revert to their primary desire to grab resources."

Gregor paused for a second. "We are going far astray," said Gregor. "I want to finish my thought on the variegations of life. Often, some people are simply born in places where they have access to more resources than other people do. These advantaged folks use their advantage to become even more advantaged. Soon, society reaches a bifurcation point where the advantaged turn the disadvantaged into slaves."

"Your capitalism facilitates the concentration of power in a few?"

"How do you mean?" asked Gregor.

"Isn't hogging resources one of the defining characteristics of capitalism?" Isn't that what is meant by the phrase bourgeois pig?" Inchoate asked.

"Hogging resources is a defining characteristic of greed, and anyone who believes in that is simply a pig," Gregor said. "Capitalism is the system where people own capital goods and run their businesses in a marketplace with little government interference."

"You believe this system enhances creativity?" asked Inchoate

"Yes, because people have more choice about what they can do for a living. When people like what they are doing, they are much more likely to work hard and be innovative," said Gregor.

"Yes, but under capitalism, people are also free to be pigs, are they not?" Inchoate said.

"What do you mean?" Gregor asked.

"I mean some people simply want power over everyone around them, and these people slowly infringe on the rights of others," explained Inchoate.

"True," said Gregor, "but capitalism actually helps to thwart these people from obtaining total dominance. Capitalism shatters the source of power into millions of pieces. Innovation diversifies enterprises, skill-sets, ownership of land and property. The hodgepodge of the capitalistic masses balances themselves."

"Are you saying that more diversification enhances dignity?" asked Inchoate

"Yes," said Gregor.

"Do you say a greater variety of vocations to choose from is best for human society?"

"Yes," said Gregor.

"Do you claim that a greater variety of products for people to choose from benefits human society?" Inchoate asked.

"Of course," said Gregor.

"You're not the least bit worried that capitalism will undermine the democratic ideal from which you have borrowed all your tired clichés?" quipped Inchoate

"No, capitalism enhances democracy."

"I think I know where you're going with this," said Inchoate.

"I doubt that," said Gregor with a laugh.

rootlet 6.14 — political energy

"Well let me try," said Inchoate. "You were going to point out that the United States is, made up of states and districts. You would say that the great variegation of the capitalistic U.S. economy ensures that the states and districts have different needs. Am I right so far?" asked Inchoate.

"Very impressive," said Gregor. What else was I going to say?"

"You were going to say that those districts and states elect politicians to represent their individual needs. So, for example, Iowa grows a lot of corn, therefore, the constituents would elect someone to represent their agricultural needs. Hawaii has a lot of tourism; therefore, the Hawaiian constituents would elect someone to represent their tourism needs. You would say that capitalism creates diverse constituents who then elect diverse representatives. In turn, you would say, the great diversity of the representatives would provide our government with eternal checks and balances."

Gregor was very impressed. "You're good," he said.

"Can you tell me Gregor, would democracy become impossible if the only commodity the United States produced was wheat?" Inchoate asked.

"Yes, I think that's true. If all the United States produced was wheat, then the division into states and districts would have little meaning. Wheat would decide who sat in Congress. Wheat would decide who presided over the courts. Wheat would choose who would be the president. Eventually, the power-hungry would seize control of the wheat and control the entire country," said Gregor.

"What do you suppose would happen to such a country?" asked Inchoate

"Such a country," said Gregor "would quickly disintegrate into extreme poverty and oppression. Eventually there would be two classes: The rare few who would live in opulent wealth, and the masses who would work under the few in condition of wretched poverty."

"Lucky for you, Gregor, that the United States has a diverse economy," said Inchoate. The United States is nowhere near this wretched state—right?" asked Inchoate.

"Fortunately not," responded Gregor.

"Even so," said Inchoate. "Could there be a commodity in your country that's very omnipresence somewhat undermines your democracy?"

"You mean like Coca-Cola?" asked Gregor.

"Well, Coke is omnipresent, but people don't have to drink Coke. I'm thinking of a commodity, that for all practical purpose, people can't refuse. Perhaps something the same color as Coke." Gregor had been so intently thinking about capitalism, he was stuck in a little conceptual shoe box. He was sure the answer had to be a drug or some kind of addictive substance.

"Coffee?" he guessed.

"No not coffee," said Inchoate impatiently. "Something black like coffee, but that is non-renewable as well."

Gregor still could not think of the answer.

"Something non-renewable, black, and that like coffee provides energy!" said Inchoate

Gregor's face reddened. "Oil," he said sheepishly.

"Yes, oil" said Inchoate.

"We already know that oil addiction is the problem," said Gregor. "We have just talked ourselves around in a giant circle."

"No, you know differently. You know the problem is that you have an energy monarchy, and oil happened to be king. People often talk about the consequences of oil: They talk about the pollution, the fluctuating costs, the unsavory people and faraway lands with which they must deal with to obtain more. They never speak of oil's most damning consequence of all—the complete erosion of economic diversity. They never speak of how oil centralizes power. Oil has elected presidents, appointed judges and controlled large portions of your congress. Oil has simplified your economy and weakened your democracy. Oil's dominance has concentrated power in the hands of a few.

"But let's forget about oil for a moment," said Inchoate. "Suppose the entire world's predominant energy was nuclear energy. Do you know what the result of that would be?"

"I suppose we would hear less about the Middle East," Inchoate said.

"You would hear nothing about the Middle East." Inchoate replied. "Instead, you would hear about countries with large uranium deposits such as Canada and Australia. You would hear that those countries hated American's freedom and loved suppression. You would hear that these countries were using their uranium to build nuclear bombs, that they were supporting evil-doers. Inevitably, the leaders of the United States would tell us that they had no choice but to invade Canada or Australia or both.

"And Gregor, do you know what would happen if arctic ice was the main source of the worlds energy?" Inchoate asked.

Gregor laughed. "I suppose we would hear how the Inuit hated American's freedom, how they were communists, or terrorists, or evil-doers. I suppose reports would leak that the Eskimos had captured Santa Claus and were torturing him in their secret ice cave. I suppose we would hear how the Eskimos were hoarding weapons and that they were planning to attack us. Eventually, the United States would say that they had no choice but to invade the North Pole and eliminate the threat."

"So now you see Gregor," said Inchoate. My imagined country of wheat is not to unlike your world of oil. Do not think that simply replacing oil will solve the problem.

"Your perspective makes a solution seem even more difficult," said Gregor,

"Why?"

"Because," said Gregor. "Alternative energy is much more expensive than oil. Developing just one economically viable alternative would be difficult enough, but to develop several would be impossible. The government has already spent hundreds of millions, perhaps billions of dollars into developing solar energy alone," replied Gregor.

"Yes," said Inchoate. The reason solar energy is expensive is the same reasons why most alternative energy is expensive."

"Which is?"

"Well," said Inchoate. "Solar cells are expensive, because they are comprised of pure silicone. Silicone requires huge amounts of heat energy to refine from the earth."

"Are you saying the massive amount of heat energy is what makes pure silicon expensive?" asked Gregor.

"Yes," said Inchoate. "Aluminum for windmills, carbon composites for light weight cars—materials like that require massive amounts of energy to refine from the earth."

All the intellectual talk was tiring Gregor. Despite his curiosity, he was getting overwhelmed and discouraged. "Perhaps there is no solution to oil addiction," he said wearily.

"Sometimes the closer one is to an answer, the more unlikely the answer seems," said Inchoate.

"More cryptic remarks," Hectic said with a sigh.

"You have climbed the rope almost to the top and now your arms burn. You only have a very short ways to go before you see the solution. Just listen a little while longer and I will furnish you with the answer. I will not ask you any more questions. All you need to do is listen to what I say," Inchoate said.

"Are we really near the end?" Gregor asked.

"Very near," replied Inchoate.

"Okay," Gregor sighed, "I'm listening."

rootlet 6.15 — Inchoate's alternative energy idea

"Human beings need to be aware of those materials that are most important to utilize alternative energy. Then, they need to do everything they can to make those materials cheap."

"Why not make all materials cheap?" asked Gregor.

"Because creating the infrastructure to economically harvest just two or three energy intensive commodities is going to be a huge sacrifice for society," Inchoate answered. "Three of the most important materials for alternative energy are silicon, aluminum and carbon composites. These three compounds share one characteristic; they all require massive amounts of energy in the form of heat and electricity to refine from the earth. Most of the heat used in this process is wasted. Humans must minimize the wasteful transfer of energy from one form to another and simplify the infrastructure on a grand scale. They must put electrical generation and refining in the same location."

"You mean you want electrical generation and the refinement of those three materials in the same facility—but why?" asked Gregor.

"I should be clear," replied Inchoate. "I speak only of the electrical generation that involves using heat to transform water into steam. I do not mean power plants that create electricity through hydroelectric or wind power."

"Most electrical power plants generate huge amounts of heat that heat water into steam. The steam then passes through a turbine and creates electricity. In that process, most of the energy is lost through waste heat. Instead of using all of the heat to turn water to steam, use a percent of that heat to refine the materials directly. Then, use the combined waste heat from the electrical generation and refining processes to heat a city," said Inchoate

"A city!" said Gregor. "What are you talking about?"

"The sacrifice society must make is that they must put this hybrid facility next to or in a city with a relatively cold climate," said Inchoate.

"Why?" asked Gregor.

"Because," said Inchoate. "A cold-climate city could best utilize the waste heat for heating buildings and water."

"Is that even possible?" asked Gregor.

"Of course," said Inchoate. "In Boston, the waste steam from electrical power plants travels through a network of pipes and heats the city. A hybrid refinery/electrical generation facility in a cold-climate city would produce energy-intensive products at a drastically cheaper price."

Gregor looked shocked. "You want to move refineries and power plants around as if they were toy blocks," he said.

"Not move," said Inchoate, "build from scratch."

"And you recommend putting this facility in the midst of an urban area?" Gregor asked, incredulous.

"Yes," answered Inchoate, "and I also recommend building a complementary transportation network that will deliver the raw ore cheaply to that facility."

"Are you crazy?" Gregor asked. "Do you think millions of people in New York City would get up and leave just so you can build your mega facility?"

"I wouldn't recommend New York City," said Inchoate. "I would recommend an urban area that has suffered economic devastation."

"You mean like the Detroit area?" asked Gregor

"Yes, Detroit would be a viable location," answered Inchoate. "The residents of Detroit might welcome a new economic engine to replace the flagging auto industry."

"Who will pay for your grandiose rearrangement?" Gregor asked.

"I can't know or dictate that," said Inchoate. "My inclination is to say that the federal government should pay to set up the infrastructure for private companies who would then take over after that."

"Don't you worry that we might be concentrating too much power into the hands of government?" asked Gregor.

"Well, maybe." Inchoate laughed. "As for whose hands you would be putting to much power in, I'm not really sure. Lately, the line between government and corporate power in the human world is quite blurry."

"You know what," said Gregor. "I don't think you're sure your idea will work."

"Certainty is for the ants," replied Inchoate. "If you want to fully regain your human form, you must embrace the chaos."

OFFSHOOT SEVEN

THE MANDELBROT SET

Inchoate inhaled a monstrous breath, lifted his head to the sky and blew out a geyser of scorching smoke. For several minutes the smoke erupted towards the sky like ash from a volcano. When he finally stopped, Inchoate had blanketed the entire sky in blackness. At first, Gregor could see nothing. Then, particles within the burning smoke sparked to life like stars and illuminated the plateau with pinpricks of light.

Inchoate turned to Gregor, "Don't let people rely on politicians and pundits to tell them what to think," he warmed. "Don't let ordinary people think they are too unqualified, powerless or stupid to come up with a solution." Inchoate reached to the heavens, curled his handpaws into semi-closed fists and began moving them as if he was pulling on an invisible rope. Above, the smoke began to attenuate downward in massive columns. The columns branched into increasingly smaller attenuations like the roots of a massive tree spreading into the ground. The first wave of black roots fell beyond the cliff. Those roots diffused into each as they stretched down and formed a black wall. The next wave of roots, landed in the vineyard. The searing smoke instantly desiccated the lush vegetation and ignited an insatiable wildfire. A tsunami of flames rose from the vineyard and advanced towards Gregor and Inchoate. Above them, the third wave of deadly roots was only a few seconds from touching down where they were.

"We must act now." yelled Inchoate. Gregor and Inchoate sprinted towards the western horizon and leapt of the cliff towards the blackness. As Gregor flew through the air, he instinctively turned his back to the wall of smoke to prevent his face from burning. He felt an intense flash of heat, and then he was on the other side of the inky veil. What he saw on the other side of the veil was so astounding that even time stopped to look. The plateau was gone. Below him, was a massive tree engulfed in flames. Gregor was sure the dying tree's name was Mandelbrot, but he did not know why he thought that. The burning of Mandelbrot released pigments that infused the smoke. Plumes of psychedelic smoke mushroomed upward and blanketed the sky like an arabesque carpet. In the center of this carpet was a black bug like shape. *That is Mandelbrot set in the sky*, thought Gregor.

Time began to lazily shift. Gregor and Inchoate reached the apex of their jump and exploded into a plume of smoke. The plume hovered for a moment before coalescing into the gray image of a man. For a moment, the ashy man remained frozen in space against the backdrop of the Mandelbrot set. He stretched his arms and legs out as if trying to reach the colors surrounding the black bug. Iridescent vapors dissolved from the set and enveloped the ashy man in a nimbus. Within the nimbus, the ashy man clarified into Gregor.

Time regained full movement. Gregor began to plummet towards the valley, and certain death, miles below. However, he did not die. Toward the end of his descent, he hit the top branches of a mighty tree. The branch bent and slowed his descent. Underneath the top branch was a descending row of several hundred branches. Each branch on the row slowed Gregor's descent further, until he landed in a deep stream near the trunk of the tree unharmed. He felt his feet hit the stream bottom and stood up. He was just tall enough that his head came out of the water.

Standing on the banks of the stream was an earthy red-haired woman holding a plate of roast beef and butter-topped mashed potatoes. On a knoll behind her, the top of the sun was just visible over the roof of a farmhouse. The butter on the potatoes was the same shade of yellow as the sun, the home was the same shade of red as the woman's hair, and the vapors rising from the dish matched the smoke wafting from the home's chimney wisp for wisp. Pollyanna Samsa smiled, knelt down and extended the dish to Gregor. "Your meat and potatoes are ready," she said.

Gregor was reaching for the dish when an excruciating pain tore through the back of his neck. The food, woman and farmhouse vanished. Gregor came to and began to choke on oily sea water. During the Deepwater Horizon tragedy, he had leapt from the oil platform and badly injured himself. He had only survived, because he had managed to clamber upon a huge buoyant tree branch with numerous little offshoots that were easy for him to grasp. After surviving the entire night adrift, he succumbed to exhaustion and slipped of the branch. He had been unconscious face down in the water. His legs had bent at the hips, as he had begun to sink feet first. In a few more seconds, he would have slipped underwater and drown. At that moment, a vulture had swooped from the sky and clawed his neck. The pain had shocked Gregor back into consciousness, and he used his last bit of energy to clamber back upon the branch. He no longer had the strength to grasp the smaller offshoots. All he could do was balance on the trunk. With all his energy gone, he knew he only had a short while to live. At any time, a wave could jostle him off the branch. The sun was just beginning to rise, and Gregor raised his head to take his last look at the Dawn. Against the backdrop of the sun, he saw a little red boat in the distance. Somebody was on the deck scanning the water, but they did not see him. Above his head, the vulture began to circle and squawk incessantly. The person turned towards the commotion and began to jump up and down. "Gregor!" she yelled. "Hang on!" The boat chugged towards Gregor. He could see her now. Above, the vulture had been circling the whole time. When Pollyanna Samsa finally grasped Gregor's hand, the vulture began circling ever higher. Finally, he disappeared into the black bug of the Mandelbrot set.

About The Dedication

Felix Brow was a 29 year old artist and designer living in New York when he passed away from Biphasic Pleural Mesothelioma, a rare cancer caused by asbestos exposure. Creativity echoed throughout Felix's brief life, bringing his unique perspective to even the most mundane of things. He had an appreciation for the offbeat and avant-garde starting at a young age. While homeschooling in middle school and high school, Felix's respect for the interconnectedness of life deepened as he took an interdisciplinary approach to learning. He had a particular interest in literature that explored math and science, preferring to learn these subjects in a creative way.

Learn more about Felix at findingfelixmemorial.blogspot.com

ONE LAST THING...

If you enjoyed this book I'd be very grateful if you'd post a short review on Amazon. Your support really does make a difference and I read all the reviews personally. I welcome the opportunity to engage in discussions of the themes explored in Mandelbrot the Tree.

Join the Discussion at mandelbrotthetree.blogspot.com

Thanks again for your support!

Made in United States
North Haven, CT
04 October 2025